MAGNOLIA

Lisa Greer

ROMANCE

BookStrand
www.BookStrand.com

A SIREN-BOOKSTRAND TITLE
IMPRINT: Romance

MAGNOLIAN
Copyright © 2011 by Lisa Greer

ISBN-10: 1-61034-505-3
ISBN-13: 978-1-61034-505-7

First Printing: April 2011

Cover design by Jinger Heaston
All cover art and logo copyright © 2011 by Siren Publishing, Inc.

Printed in the U.S.A.

PUBLISHER
www.BookStrand.com

DEDICATION

To Stephen for asking the question...

MAGNOLIAN

LISA GREER

Chapter 1

Oh for a draught of vintage! that hath been Cool'd a long age in the deep-delv'd earth...
—from "Ode to a Nightingale" by John Keats

The autumn wind always cut through bone like a surgical knife, but today it was especially incisive as she stood against it, her long hair unfurling behind her. On the edge of Berry Creek Cemetery, bony trees waved stiffly in the breeze like standing dead men. A single crimson leaf fluttered in front of her and landed on one of her black pumps. Gazing sightlessly down at the gilt-edged coffin, lowered over the blue-tarp-outlined hole, she shivered and drew her gray coat tightly about her. The start of November was an especially cruel time to die here in the Northeast. The turning was over, and most of the leaves were dried husks, only memories of vibrant life and color. Lillian gazed out in front of her, past the few mourners and the ramrod figure of the minister, at the marbled stones jutting out of the cold ground, so many of them resting on the hill above her. She had loved this cemetery with its rows of old, white and gray marbled headstones. Her father had often reminded her that generations of Mullinses were buried there, back to 1755. The thought of him resting there—her daddy—under the snow that was threatening to blanket everything here, even this evening, made her knees tremble.

"Brothers and sisters." The minister swept his arm dramatically across himself. "We know now that for those predestined to be His, they are resting with Him and will not—cannot!—be taken out of His hands." The scowling Presbyterian minister, impossibly erect and clothed in all black with a matching dark scar on his cheek, droned on, brows furrowed. Her father would have laughed with her if only he could have heard his send off. By a twist of fate, the previous minister of Grace Presbyterian Church in Pittsburgh had passed away just months before, during her father's illness. The very Reverend and very Scottish Donald MacDuff was filling in for him in the church. That job included funerals with a firm Calvinist viewpoint. Her own father had been a man of faith, but his faith was gentler. He always said that he would have been a Quaker if he had not been born in Pittsburgh to a staunch Calvinist theologian for a father and a hard-line Presbyterian church woman for a mother.

Lillian, in a daze, realized the funeral was over. She dropped a single white rose on her father's casket, sucking surreptitiously at her thumb, where a thorn had pierced the skin as she clenched it during the minister's rambling oration. She had bought the rose up the road a few days ago with her father in mind. A few friends from school—two girls from the English department in college that she had gone out with for drinks and just chatted with in general, and one from her Victorian Period English class at Pitt—were there and passed by to give her hugs and murmured reassurances that they were thinking about her. She was a senior at the University of Pittsburgh after a transfer from Berkeley before her junior year, when her father had taken a very good position here. She knew her friends who had bothered to come today were thinking of her and wanted to help—for the moment, and then they wouldn't anymore. After all, what could she expect as a girl who had spent only a year here in the suburbs of Pittsburgh and a year at the University of Pittsburgh as an English major?

Her father had pined for Pittsburgh after thirty years away in San Francisco. He had always told her that he loved green trees, green grass, and hills. She had hesitated about following him from California, but in the end, she had known it was the right thing to do. He was so alone, and she had never lived anywhere else. It had turned out to be the right choice, especially now that he was gone so soon. She also had found that she liked Pittsburgh, as different as it was from the West Coast.

Her father had taught at Carnegie Mellon for six months before he received a cancer diagnosis. He was given no hope from the outset—stage three pancreatic cancer. He had hoped against hope and enjoyed his life as much as he could until he got too sick to hike, ride his bike, or go on trips to see Falling Water or the Amish in Lancaster, Pennsylvania, with her. They had promised each other to squeeze all that they could out of those last days, and she thought they had succeeded, which made his death a bit easier. He had smiled at one point after he was in bed for the duration and told her he had crossed off ninety percent of his "Things to Do Before I Die List." She had been afraid to ask about the other ten percent. She didn't want to cry anymore.

Lillian had stayed by his side, nursing him when she wasn't in classes, holding his feverish hand in the last days and reading Keats and Shelley to him as hospice nurses walked back and forth, in and out, taking care of his needs. "Ode to a Nightingale" elicited a special response for him in those days when he would gasp in attempted laughter, asking for a draught of vintage. After some weeks of nursing him, she dropped out of college mid-semester of her senior year, overwhelmed and needing a break. She knew she had little time left with her father, and she wanted to spend it at his side. He died just three weeks later. At only fifty-eight, he had died too young, and his bright smile and imposing personality were seared on Lillian's mind. Her mother had had her when she was twenty-five—scandalously married to her professor for a short time. The two of them had been truly in love. Her father often told her that he had never loved another woman until he had met her mother, Gretchen, in his Keats seminar. Lillian found that hard to believe, but she knew her father would never lie about matters of the heart. His serious nature was a part of him that she loved.

Just days before his death, his periwinkle blue eyes still glittering with soft memory, he struggled to tell the story again. "And in she walked to the lecture hall at Berkeley—late. Her golden hair flashed under the hot lights of the auditorium as a book thudded to the floor in her rush to a seat. I've still never seen hair the color of hers—or yours. You know, you have that same titian hair. Anyway, she was a wisp—ethereal even from where I was standing some twenty feet away on stage. I knew then that I had to meet her." He did as soon as the first lecture was over, making sure to catch her before she slipped out of the door. They had coffee in a shop a little distance away from campus so as not to cause undue gossip and talked about the Romantics and her thesis work thus far on Shelley's philosophy of science. They disagreed vehemently, and he was smitten. Three months later, he asked her to marry him. She did. They set up house, and she taught part time at Berkeley after finishing her thesis. Two years later, Lillian was born.

Lillian turned from the grave site as the last of the mourners paid their respects. She was hugged and hand-shaken out, she thought. She was simply relieved that there would be nothing else at her home that evening that she had to deal with.

With a curt nod to the minister, she began walking on shaky legs back toward her home, just a half mile away. She hadn't trusted herself to drive her father's Honda today to the church. The funeral home had picked her up in a limousine that she rode in, breath puffing and tears welling in her eyes. She had arranged to walk home alone. She needed the time for reflection and didn't want to ride home in a limousine. As she walked under the fleur de lis of the rust-speckled high archway that pronounced Berry Hill Cemetery in white letters, she felt a hand on her shoulder. She gasped softly, having been lost in her own world.

When she turned, she recognized Donovan Ross, the church pianist and organist at Grace Presbyterian. He was still and quiet, as usual, and a lock of wavy blue-black hair falling across his forehead drew attention to his crystalline green eyes. They had been the first thing she had noticed about him her second Sunday at the church months ago. She remembered the Gulf of Mexico near where her mother's family lived, and she knew the hue of his eyes matched that sea—blue-green and changeable. In her first Sunday at the church last summer, she had noticed other things about him, too, like his long, thin fingers playing over the keys, his straight but powerful back, and his full lips that pulled into a half smile as he played Bach. When he stood up in mid-service she had nearly gasped at his height—better than six feet and graceful in every inch of that. Her seat at the left side in front of the church had been one from which she could worship— mainly Donovan and not God. She had learned through the pastor's discussion with her father early on that Donovan had just graduated from Grove City College with his music degree and was something of a prodigy. He had taken the post at the church in order to work on his graduate studies in Pittsburgh.

"Hi, Lillian. I didn't mean to startle you," Donovan said with his quiet voice—the kind of voice that made women want to listen because it seemed he must have something profound to say since he did not choose to speak up or yell as so many men did. She listened hard as she always had when he was speaking—usually it was not to her but to others.

"Oh, no, you didn't startle me. Thanks for coming. It means more than I can say that you're here." Lillian could feel her heart thudding as they stood together under the arch of the entrance, the sun beginning to set in the west—a ball of lukewarm fire on a rare, sunny autumn afternoon. The sunset felt like the end to a long day, but she knew the day wasn't over yet. There was still the long night to get through.

He smiled at her. "I wouldn't have missed paying my respects. Your father was a wonderful man. I enjoyed all our talks about music in the twentieth century." Donovan shoved his hair behind his ear as he talked.

"Oh, I know he felt the same. He loved to have a bright young guy to talk to—as he put it. He went on and on about your playing at church. He said he was thankful he had never gone to one of those "praise chorus churches" as he put it." Lillian shoved her fists in the pockets of her coat awkwardly and stamped her feet a little against the numbness that was growing in them from prolonged standing and the cold air.

"Where are you going now?" Donovan asked in a rush, glancing sideways rather than right into her eyes. She realized he must be nervous, and it surprised her for some reason. He was older than her, so she thought he wouldn't feel the same way she did at times— awkward and unsure.

"I'm walking home. I live just a half mile down the road." Lillian's stomach teemed with sudden butterflies. She wondered if he was just being polite—making small talk with a lonely girl who had no one as evidenced by only a stream of college mourners and the odd old friend here and there who had to catch a plane back before the new week began. She did have no one—here anyway. All her family was in Alabama—from her mother's side. And that was only a middle-aged aunt and her Grandmother Stark, who was too feeble to make it to the funeral. Anyone else who was family was unknown— no close cousins or anyone else who cared about her. A sudden sob threatened to burst from her throat. She swallowed it down, angry with herself. She was going to have to get tough fast if she was going to survive—emotionally anyway. She couldn't be crying every time a sad thought came into her head.

Donovan must have seen her face change because he touched her arm lightly, shifting his legs. "Why don't you come with me? I know a good coffee shop a few miles away. You don't have to talk—just have whatever hot drink you want." He smiled slightly. "You look like you could use some unthawing, and I know I could. Fall is definitely here to stay." He looked around as he said it at the barren treetops and the bed of leaves on the ground.

"Honestly, that sounds wonderful," Lillian said, not thinking before the words came out. Once she had said it, she wondered how great it would be—for him anyway. Spending time with her right now would be a real blast, as sad as she was. She took a tremulous breath and tried to pull herself together. There would be time for more crying later.

He took her arm in his and led her toward his car—a battered blue Hyundai parked near the cemetery entrance. It was the last car there. Everyone else had left, and there were no visitors to other graves on a cold day like today. It was hard enough to visit the dead when the sun was shining and it was warm.

He motioned toward his car with his hand. "It's not a chariot, but it gets me from here to there." He opened the door for her, and she slumped into the seat, suddenly feeling drained of energy and thought.

Donovan must have sensed her mood, she thought, because he drove without a word to the coffee shop in Penn Hills—a cheery but quiet and private little place. The last rays of the sunset flamed in the sky, leaving trails of peach and baby pink.

They got out of the car quickly and hoofed it into the warm shop. Donovan handed her into a booth in the corner, and they sat in silence for a moment as the lumpy, middle aged waitress padded over to take their order.

After ordering Chai teas and a small plate of buttery blueberry scones, they lapsed into further silence. It was not uncomfortable—just natural. Lillian's eyelids drooped a bit as the effects of two days with little sleep hit. She perked up when the waitress brought two steaming cups of Chai and a plate of buttery scones.

"I really appreciate your doing this. I'm glad I didn't have to go home to the quiet house. I haven't been sleeping too well. I think I might sleep tonight, though." She smiled at him over her steaming cup as she nibbled a scone.

He shrugged. "No problem. I wanted to get to know you a little better. I'm always busy at church, and with your dad being sick these last few months, I haven't seen you there in a while." Donovan leaned toward her slightly as she spoke, and she noticed his eyes again. She didn't remember ever meeting a man with eyes like that. She could get lost in them and forget what she was talking about.

"Hmm. Well, about me. I guess there's not much to tell really." Lillian's tongue felt thick and slow in her mouth. "I dropped out of college a little while ago when my father got really sick. He urged me not to do it, but I—I just couldn't seem to focus on school. I mean, I knew he wasn't going to make it at that point, and school could wait, you know? There were too many things I wanted to do with him, and we did a lot of them before he got too sick to go." She looked down into her tea cup, collecting herself. "I miss college, but it was the right thing to do. I know that now for sure." She took a sip of tea.

"Don't be too hard on yourself. I lost my parents when I was six. They died in a plane crash over the Grand Canyon—sightseeing. It changed my life when I moved here to live with my uncle. Sometimes I'd give anything to see them again—just to talk with them one time." He stopped with obvious emotion and took a sip of his tea. "I don't know why I'm talking about this. Anyway, the point is I know you did the right thing—spending those last days with your father." Donovan splayed his hands on the table and sighed, his eyes darkening to glimmering emeralds.

"Oh. I had no idea—about your parents, I mean. I'm so—sorry," Lillian said, clasping her hands nervously on the table. She picked up her scone and took a bite—more to have something to do with her hands than because she was really hungry. Donovan's grief from so many years ago brought into the present made hers feel small. She couldn't imagine not knowing either parent for more than a few years and being orphaned at such a young age. Tears gathered in her eyes again for her loss and for his. She felt an instant connection to him—like none she had ever felt with anyone apart from her father. She knew they would be friends if not more, though she felt silly even thinking that. She had no real knowing about anything in her life right now, but somehow she knew this.

Donovan reached out and cupped her hands in his. "I'm fine. It was years ago. It just changed who I was, who I am—all of me really—to lose them. So I know how you must be feeling. Will you stay here in the area for school and in your home? If you need anything—" he stopped, and his sharp cheekbones flushed as he released her hands slowly.

"I'm fine. I probably will stay here. I don't know where else I'd go," Lillian said with a sharp bark of laughter that sounded like a groan. "Besides, the house is paid for. Dad left an insurance policy and other money. So, I can stay there—or not. I have a lot of things to figure out." She took a deep breath.

"And plenty of time to figure them out," Donovan said so that she had to listen to hear him. He took the last scone from the plate and popped half of it into his mouth, making her smile in spite of her sadness.

"Yes." She ate her last bite of scone, wishing she could prolong the evening but knowing she was too exhausted to actually do so.

"It looks like you're about to fall asleep with that mug in your hand. Are you ready to go? I'll take you home and make sure you're settled for the night." Donovan helped her with her jacket as they walked out into the bone biting wind. Tears of gratitude, sadness, and exhaustion pricked her eyes and spilled down her cheeks. She wiped them away as she slid into the car, Donovan's hand warm on her shoulder as he helped her in. The drive home was in companionable silence.

They drove up the hill to the old two-story, apple-red and white-trimmed coal mining house her father had purchased for less than eighty thousand dollars a few years ago. He had beamed at her and said, "That's what you can get house-wise here in the Burgh. Try that back in California!" He loved the nostalgia of the house and its location, and he was a man of the people at his core—no fancy home for him. He and Lillian had delighted in the Sears imprint on the hardwood floors that indicated that the house was a Sears kit house, shipped by train to Pittsburgh. The modest neighborhood suited him and Lillian quite well. Lillian climbed the steps to the door wearily, Donovan close behind her. She yawned as she stood under the porch light, turning the key and opening the door.

She flipped on the lights, and the shadows fled. The silence of the house made her nervous, as it had for the past few days without her father there. The gossamer mint-green curtains in the sitting room swayed like unsteady ghosts as the air from the heater kicked on and skimmed through them.

"Here," she indicated the couch. "Please—sit down. Can I get you a glass of water or something?" She kicked off her shoes and hung up her coat on the coat rack by the door. Her shadow showed long on the opposite wall.

Donovan smiled as he leaned against the wall near the door. "No, thanks. Thanks again for your company tonight. I waited way too long to get to know you."

"Thanks—for everything." Lillian yawned again and clapped a hand over her mouth. She smiled and said, "I'm sorry. It's not your company. It's just all this—the last few days." She walked over to the apricot silk couch and sank down on the end of it.

Donovan sat near the other end of the couch, resting long fingers on his legs and looking at her.

"Well, I won't keep you up. I know you need your sleep. It's been a long day for you. If there is anything I can do, please call me. Wait. Here's my number, and I want yours, too." He pulled out a little red notebook from his back pocket.

"Wow. You're prepared for anything." She looked at the

weathered notebook in admiration.

"This is my composition notebook. I scrawl in it when I get an idea for a new song or a way I want an arrangement for an old one we're working on at the church. I know. Weird, huh? But it works for me." He smiled lopsidedly. "So, what's your number?" He cocked a dark brow at her.

Lillian gave him her number and took the slip of paper with his on it and put it on the end table by the sofa.

"All right, I'll call you some time tomorrow afternoon. I just want to check on you—if that's okay." The dulcet tones were back in his voice as he leaned toward her.

"Yes, that's fine. I mean, I'd like that. Thanks for everything." They both stood up, and Lillian walked him to the door.

"Goodnight, Lillian. Take care." Donovan touched her cheek as he stood in the half open doorway, the porch light and a full, melon-colored moon illuminating his black hair, making it shine like a raven's silken feathers, his green eyes in shadows. Lillian shivered in spite of herself as his hand ran down her cheek to her collarbone. She clasped his fingers with her hand, feeling a strange sense of loss when she looked at him. What a funny thought, she told herself.

"Good night. Thank you. Be careful going home." She released his hand as he backed away, his gaze locked on her until he pivoted to disappear down the steps and into the silvery night. After he drove away, the silence descended on the house again, making her nervous.

After she shut the door and made sure everything was locked up tight, she slowly climbed the steps to her room. Shadows played on the landing above her, and she sighed aloud. Her heart pounded at the utter silence of the house, and she avoided looking at her father's room—now straightened and cleaned by Dulcie, the twice weekly housekeeper who had come for years. Lillian still had a fear that she would look into his room and see him in the bed, his once gloriously thick brown hair limp on his forehead and blue eyes sunken into his face. She darted past his room and into hers. She closed the door and locked it for the first time in years with the little key that fit into the lock. She hurriedly stripped her black dress, pantyhose, and pumps off as well as the plain black disk earrings she had worn to the funeral.

She padded into the bathroom and washed her face and brushed her teeth hurriedly. Only after she was done did she look in the mirror. She looked like a half-dead thing with limp, shoulder-length hair framed her face—the hair her father had always loved—and violet-colored eyes ringed with dark circles stared back at her from a face that was even paler than its usual alabaster tinge. She sighed and flipped off the light, happy to cross the room and fall into bed after turning on the lamp. Reaching beside her, she grabbed her copy of *Pride and Prejudice*—a novel that would ensure sleep for her tonight. Within ten minutes, her eyes closed, and the novel slipped out of her hands. She jerked awake, flipped off the light, and oblivion descended.

The next thing she was aware of was her father's voice, "Lil... Lillian, listen." He spoke in a whisper, his face pale and drawn, brow wrinkled with worry. He seemed to float above her, and she was running on a dirt path in a white nightgown. She could feel the bite of small rocks under her bare feet; she shivered from the chill in the air. Angry voices shouted behind her as her heart pounded, feeling like it would burst from her chest. She was so afraid. Tears were rolling down her cheeks as her father kept whispering. Somehow, she looked like herself, but she didn't feel like herself. She felt younger and sleeker. She could only attribute that to being in a dream state.

Suddenly, with a gasp, she awoke to the moonlight slanting through half closed blinds. She was safe. She was home. It was only a dream, or a nightmare, as most would call it. Sitting up, she glanced at the alarm clock on her nightstand: 3:33. She shivered at the repeated numbers as if they were an ill omen. Opening her nightstand drawer, she fumbled around for a small bottle of sleeping pills she had gotten a month ago at the doctor's office. She hated to take them and had only done so twice, but tonight she needed the rest. Swallowing a pill, she lay back until her eyes closed again.

Chapter 2

I cannot see what flowers are at my feet, Nor what soft incense
hangs upon the boughs,
—from "Ode to a Nightingale" by John Keats

She awoke late to a gray sky and no sunlight through the window—another typical November day in Western Pennsylvania. Her father had disliked winter here, falling into a funk during his first winter here that only antidepressants would cure. She had never been prone to the seasonal depression that took him over, but today, she was not so sure. Her head felt like a sack full of sharp pebbles as she groaned and sat up. She stumbled into the bathroom and stood under the hot spray, feeling human again in a few minutes. In slow motion, she got dressed in a thick baby-blue sweater and jeans. It suddenly dawned on Lillian that there was no need to hurry. The thought stopped her cold as she zipped her jeans and snapped them.

It was the second of November, and her life stretched out before her—an endless series of nothing specials without her father or anyone. She couldn't imagine how her life had come to be so blank when she was so young, but then, she had always been alone, with only her father and her dreams of becoming a novelist, and if not a novelist, a good editor for great novelists. As she slipped her feet into her warm house slippers, a tiny smile came when she thought of Donovan and last night. Maybe there would not be an endless series of nothings after all. Maybe she would have a normal life like other women her age had—with a man who cared about them or the potential of such a man and a life she loved, or barring that, perhaps she would just be happy alone, finishing school and getting a job. She shook her head and muttered to herself. Lillian knew that danger lay that way—in thinking that he cared about her or that things would change suddenly for her. He was just being kind last night, as anyone would be. She was alone, and she had to start fending for herself. She squared her shoulders and decided she would tackle some paperwork her father had left behind—after a cup of strong coffee.

As she sipped her black coffee and ate warm buttered toast sitting at the old dining room table in front of the triple-paned windows that swirled with aged glass, the silence of the house spun out before her. She imagined that she heard an echo of her father's booming voice or felt his undeniable presence beside her at the table as she had so many mornings in the past. Tears pricked her eyes at the thought, and she understood, maybe for the first time, that he was not there in the house—not even his ghost. And he would not be back. He truly was under the cold winter ground at Berry Creek, and there was nothing she could do about it, just as there had been nothing she could do about losing her mother before she had the chance to know her.

She focused on the single brown squirrel skittering around the back yard among the tulip bed. What she would give to see a yellow tulip in bloom today! She and her father had so enjoyed the bed of red, yellow, and pink tulips. She had picked the yellow ones weekly just for him and placed them on a vase on this table. She had loved to see his eyes light up when he came in from a long day of lecturing and grading and saw them. He was a man of complex thoughts, but he always had time to stop and enjoy the finer things in life, no matter how small they were.

As the fog in her head cleared, she remembered her dream from the night before—her father's worried face looming over her as she ran and ran. What could the dream have meant? She had always been a sound sleeper, and when she had dreamed, luckily, her dreams were of happy memories or harmless fantasies. She didn't believe in spirits or omens from the beyond, but she couldn't shake the feeling of fear the dream had given her, even now in the morning light with the mundane things of life scattered around her and before her outside the window.

Pushing the thoughts aside, she began filling out a form to stop payment on an academic journal her father had always loved. She sighed, thinking about the many similar tasks she had to do in coming days. They stretched out before her, looking monotone and gray.

She heard a thunk outside the kitchen door: Mr. Morse had dropped off the mail in the box. How quaint it was that the mail came right to the door—all the way around the back of the house to the tiny kitchen that had likely been added on some years after the house's construction. That was one thing she liked about living here—the feeling of being in a bygone era that an old house could lend. The mail delivery was just one such reminder that people had once had mail carried to their doors. She was still one of the lucky ones, she thought with a smile, as she walked through the icy kitchen.

Welcoming the distraction, she opened the heavy wooden door, shivering in the mid-morning cold. Reaching her hand into the mailbox, she grabbed the mail and shut the door quickly, driving out the chill. Throwing the mail on the table, she pushed her paperwork aside. After looking at two bills and a letter from her father's lawyer, she saw a lavender envelope with a flowing black script which she recognized immediately as her Grand's handwriting from the many birthday cards, Easter cards, and Christmas cards she had received in her twenty-two years. They did not often talk on the phone—they had a few days ago when Lillian had called to tell her grand about her father's death and the funeral arrangements—but they sent cards to each other regularly. She slipped the letter out of the envelope with a whisper of vellum and read with a tripping heart:

October 30, 2010

Dear Lillian,

I am so sorry I was not able to fly up for your father's funeral. As you know, my health has not been so good recently, and your Aunt Lorelei's depression has worsened. I did some thinking after you called, and I want you to come to Magnolian for the rest of the year. We have a lovely community college here in Everwood where you might take some classes. There are also businesses in the area where you could intern. In other words, there is plenty to do here, and you can spend some time regaining your footing surrounded by those who love you. I have enclosed plane ticket vouchers for you to Montgomery, Alabama, any time before Thanksgiving. You are welcome to stay as long as you like. Come when you can; we'll be expecting you.

My love always,

Grand

Lillian's heart pounded in her chest, and she felt an excited flush creep up her cheeks. A letter, rather than a phone call, was just like her Grand. A lady of old fashioned ideas, Grand loved the written word and the old ways of doing things. She hadn't sent an email in her almost seventy years that Lillian knew of. She pressed the letter to her chest, already knowing what her answer to the letter would be. She hadn't been to her mother's childhood home, Magnolian, for years now—since she was twelve. That summer had been one of bliss: roaming the woods behind the old Queen Anne era house, riding her bike on the wooded paths, reading Gothic novels late into the night from Grand's huge library, and spending time talking with Grandmother or sightseeing in Everwood—the nearby, sleepy small town. She had spent many late nights chatting with Grand about life in the old days and with Grandfather Tate—Jim, as his friends called him—an imposing man with a grin that went from ear to ear in the old family photo album. He had died when Lillian was only a baby. Since that trip, life had kept her busy, and her father had needed her in summers starting when she was thirteen to help with his scholarly articles. And she had needed that work for the pay he gave her and for the experience that would be helpful for college, graduate school, and a career as a writer or editor some day. The savings account she had accrued wasn't a bad bonus either.

She calculated hurriedly that she would need a week to get the house and car taken care of—to have someone come in and check on things while she was away and a few days to make other preparations. Dulcie would surely be willing to house sit if she were offered enough money. That way, it would cover her missed housekeeping pay for the time Lillian was away. She didn't want to lose her help. Buying some less wintry clothes was on the list, too. She didn't think the autumn and winter temperatures ever hit below twenty degrees there. Her thoughts stopped short as she thought of Donovan. Would he be disappointed when she told him she was leaving for the fall—or for longer? She grimaced wryly at her silly notions of romance. She knew that her naiveté was showing in her thoughts. Having had only two boyfriends in her life, and both of those in her high school years in California, what did she know of love or even like? Her relationships with both Jack and Derek had been comprised mainly of fumblings under the stars in the backseat with her fending off unskilled advances. She had wanted more than sex and was less experienced than anyone she had known in high school—save her old friend Leanne back in California. Now, even Leanne had a boyfriend, and she had slept with him months ago. She wondered, not for the first time, if not having a mother had led to her insecurity and fear about sex, and well, about life at times. She was a hesitant person, going willy-nilly from here to there, not sure about her own dreams and goals. Her father had been the opposite, she thought, her throat thick with unshed tears.

Plopping down again at the table, Lillian decided to banish her self-pity. She found a piece of paper and began a long to-do list to prepare for the trip. The mundane affairs of her father's life were forgotten on the table. Engrossed in the growing list of things to think about before leaving her home for months on end, she almost missed the chirping of her cell phone from the kitchen counter. She sprinted to the kitchen and grabbed it without looking at the caller ID.

"Hello?" Her breath came out in a whisper as she glanced back at the table, pen still in her hand. The call had startled her in the silence of the house.

"Lillian? Hey, it's Donovan. I was just checking on you. Everything okay?" The quiet voice on the other end of the line made her knees quiver, and she quickly sat back down in the lyre-back chair in the dining room, so unexpected was the call. She had not believed he would call her as he had said he would.

"Yes, I'm fine. Doing great, well, not great, but you know. I'm just getting things done," she murmured, trying to inject a cheery note into her voice. Her face flamed at the idiocy of her response.

"Sounds good. Hey, listen. I was wondering if you'd like to get together tonight. No pressure—whatever you'd like to do. Your place, mine, some other place?" She heard the expectant silence.

"That sounds great. How about a movie? I really need to get out again, and I enjoyed last night so much. My treat tonight, of course," she rushed to add. She didn't want him to think she was a gold digger.

"Nope, it's my treat again." She heard the smile in his voice. "Otherwise, it sounds like a plan. I'll pick you up for dinner first, maybe around six? Is that okay, or do you have plans?"

She rolled her eyes. If he only knew the plans she didn't have! "No, no plans. That sounds great.

"I'll see you then." She hit the end button, disconnecting before even thinking about it and laughed under her breath. She had a date, but this would be one of the last, since she was leaving. The thought filled her with emptiness despite the promise of going to Magnolian.

Sighing, she turned to her list again and decided to go shopping after noon for clothes for the trip. She stopped a moment, wondering what her father would think. He had never been a fan of Magnolian or even of Alabama for that matter. A true Yankee, he scoffed at what he saw as the ways of the Old South that were still entrenched under a thin veil of politeness. She remembered his frowns when she told him of Grand's servants after her last visit—all black—and of the attitudes of some of the people in Everwood. He had not been to Everwood for many years. His only love there had been her mother. The rest he could leave.

"Pure racism," he had scoffed. "I can't understand why people prefer to live in the past, rather than embrace the present—not to mention the future." He had glowered when she told him in a rush of words all about her summer month in Everwood. As a twelve–year-old, she had felt a sting of disapproval. These were her mother's people—her heritage. How could he say such things? Was there something about her mother, about her family, that she didn't know?

Now, as a twenty-two-year-old, older and wiser and more educated about the Civil Rights movement and other issues, she understood her father's judgment and anger. She felt a flutter of uncertainty in her stomach. How would Everwood and Magnolian look to her now—with years passed and her own life so changed?

Cleaning up the kitchen dishes, she resolved to put these worries out of her mind. She had been overwhelmed with sadness and grief for so long. She was going to look to Magnolian as a fresh beginning—unclouded by the past.

Her drive into town with the Christmas lights newly strung and Christmas trees sprinkling certain city blocks cheered her considerably. Kaufmann's downtown was having a big sale on winter clothing, and she bought another pair of jeans, some trousers, warm socks, and a lighter jacket for the comparably balmy fall Southern nights. She also threw in a new purse and a pretty pink suitcase, using money from her joint account with her father. He had had the foresight to have her signed on a month before his death. Even the drive back through unrelenting slate skies could not steal her excitement. She tried to push down the hope bubbling up within her, but it refused to subside.

After darting up the stairs of the house when she returned, ignoring the eerie silence of the house and putting her new purchases away, she decided to lie down and rest a while before her date later that evening. She was drowsy from her night of poor sleep. As she drifted off, she feared a repeat of the previous night's dream, but she was too tired to consider staying awake. When she awoke an hour later to her alarm playing Benjamin Britten's *Requiem for War*—darn NPR on a gloomy day—she shivered slightly, pushing the off button quickly. At least the nightmare had not recurred, and she was well-rested.

Standing before her closet, she wondered what to wear. The cold night that was sure to come required a sea foam green cashmere sweater—a gift from her father earlier this year—and a pair of forest-green corduroy pants. A pair of brown suede boots completed the ensemble. Lillian brushed her hair—letting its layers fall toward her face. She had never believed in high-maintenance hair, so the inverted layered cut suited her slightly round face well. She put a light dash of peach blush on and a rosy lip gloss, blue eyeliner to call attention to her violet eyes, and blond brow makeup for her almost invisible brows, and she was ready to go. She walked downstairs and picked up her copy of *Northanger Abbey* from her father's study to pass the fifteen minutes until Donovan's arrival and to still her fluttering heart. She smiled, realizing she was always reading at least three books at a time—a habit she had learned from her father, who was a voracious reader. They had both walked around with a book in hand on Saturday mornings. The thought brought a lump to her throat.

Promptly at six p.m., the doorbell rang. Standing from her perched place on the couch and taking a deep breath, Lillian grabbed her purse, smoothed her hair, and opened the door. Donovan was standing there, striking as always with a pink polo-style shirt peeking out from under a dark leather coat. His long legs were shown to advantage in khaki slacks. He led her down the steps along the sidewalk to his Hyundai. They hurried along to avoid the chill.

"I was thinking Squirrel Hill for dinner and the movie? Sound good?" He asked as he helped her in to the car. Her hand brushed his, and a tingle ran through her.

"That sounds great," she answered truthfully as she shut his door.

They drove in silence for the first few minutes.

"So, how was your day?" Lillian asked, clearing her throat.

Donovan frowned. "It was okay. I've had better. We had practice this afternoon for the Christmas Eve music service, and it was hell. Mrs. Martin's solo sounds like a dying bird's squawk, and I just can't seem to get my organ parts correct. I need a break. Thank God the semester will be over in a few weeks, and I can have a break from school for the holidays. That will take some of the stress off, but the musical must go on." He smiled and looked at her, light from the street lamps glinting off of his jade eyes.

"How about your day? Did you sleep okay?" he asked, looking at her with concern as he drove through darkening streets as dusk fell.

"Not really. I had a bad dream—a weird dream. I took a sleeping pill—didn't want to, but I figured it would at least help me get some rest." Lillian clamped her lips together, not wanting to talk about the dream.

Donovan sensed her reticence. "Well, if you want to talk about it, I'm here, but for now, it's good times. We're at my favorite Thai place. Have you ever been here?" He pulled the car smoothly into a metered space in Squirrel Hill, and they got out.

Lillian had not been to Tuy's before, and she enjoyed the spiced Thai fish and shrimp tremendously as well as the good conversation and mod black and silver design of the place. When she was with Donovan, it seemed, things were lighter and easier. They walked from the restaurant to a feel-good film about wacky college friends, and Lillian was smiling when she left the theater. The film was not her usual cup of tea, but she had needed something light tonight. Donovan seemed to be able to read her moods, and she appreciated his deference to them, especially right now while she felt fragile. She was determined not to stay that way, but it was good to have someone to lean on—just a little.

They held hands as they walked back to the car. Donovan raised her palm to kiss it tenderly as he opened the door for her. She slid inside and took a deep breath in the dark interior, wondering if she should tell him that she was going to be leaving for Alabama in just a week and a half if she could get everything done by then.

"Donovan?" His name came out as a soft question on her lips, and she suddenly felt young and frightened again, the bright lights, happy city dwellers, and bubblegum movie erased from her mind as they drove the black streets over the bridge and out of the city toward the suburbs.

"Yes, what is it?" His long fingers gripped the wheel as he turned slightly to her, dark hair hiding part of his face in shadow.

"I don't even know why I'm telling you this or making a big deal out of it. It probably won't matter anyway, but—" she stuttered on, biting her lip and tasting blood.

"What? If it's about you, it certainly matters to me." Donovan's soft voice held conviction, and her heart did a slow somersault.

"Well, I got a letter from my grandmother in Alabama today, and she's invited me to stay with her for a while—just to get away and think. And I'm going—in the next week or so," Lillian said with a hitch in her voice. Why did she think he should care? He barely knew her.

"Oh." Donovan pulled up to the curb in front of her house and turned the car off. "To be honest, I wish you weren't leaving. I'm just getting to know you." He smiled and touched her hand, trailing his fingers down to hers as she shivered. "But it sounds like a trip that would be good for you."

"I think it will," Lillian said.

"Can I come in?" His eyes shone like leaping green flames, and she felt hot all over.

"Sure."

They walked up the looming shadowed sidewalk and steps. Suddenly, the motion sensor light sprang on. Lillian unlocked the door. She could feel Donovan close behind her, a reassuring presence she had not experienced for some time since her father's illness began.

"I wouldn't leave now, normally. I'd just start school again or do—something. It's just that I need to get away. I can't stand the silence here since dad died." She threw her purse down on the couch. "Can I get you something to drink?" She kicked her boots off and hung her jacket up as she turned to Donovan.

"Yes, please—just some water." He sat down on the couch, looking at her.

She flushed and turned away, moving quickly through the dark dining room and into the kitchen, flipping on the light and stilling her breathing as she let the water dispense from the freezer door.

"So, when do you leave?" She heard his voice from the sitting room.

She carried two cups of ice-cold water into the sitting room, jumping a little as the old furnace kicked on and heat brushed against her ankles.

"Hopefully in seven days."

"Well! You seem to know your own mind. That's good." Donovan smiled and took a sip of his water. "I guess I'll just have to make the most of that seven days. I've wasted so much time already, thinking you would never want to spend time with me." He moved closer to her on the couch, his eyes as mysterious as a forest at dusk.

"What?" Lillian couldn't help the question when it came. She laughed. "I thought the same of you. The first time I saw you—up in the organ loft, you seemed almost otherworldly—an angel without the wings. I know it's corny, but it's true." She dipped her head, not able to meet his gaze. She wasn't sure why things were moving so quickly between them. The only theory that made sense was that he had been there for her the day of her father's funeral, and that had bonded her to him—and likewise.

He laughed softly, lifting her chin with his long fingers and looking straight into her eyes until she felt warm all over. When he kissed her, it felt like nothing she had experienced to that point. She could understand skyrockets, stars, explosions. She felt those feelings as he moved closer and embraced her, more insistent with his kiss.

She broke away from him with a gasp, straightening her sweater.

"I'm sorry. It's just that—" She stopped, at a loss for words, feeling foolish and young again.

He laughed again. "I know. I won't move so fast. You're leaving, and I don't want to confuse you. You need time for yourself to sort things out. It's just that I know what I want already, no sorting needed." He winked at her and put his arm around her shoulder.

"Thanks for understanding." She leaned against his arm, and they spent the rest of the evening talking until well into the wee hours of the morning. Lillian was in no rush for him to leave. It was Sunday night, and the next day held countless errands and before that, the night threatened nightmares and voices from the grave. She shook her head to clear it. She was acting like a soap-opera character, dramatic and silly, she chided herself in her head.

The goodnight kiss was lingering, and Lillian closed the door feeling a bit depressed as she turned to mount dark steps to go to bed.

The night passed uneventfully, and bright sunlight awoke her the next morning. She got up and wrote a quick response letter to Grand telling her to expect her on November tenth. She popped the letter into the mailbox as she sailed around the house, getting ready to leave to run errands. After coffee and oatmeal, she got dressed hurriedly and headed out to the bank to withdraw money for the trip and get new checks with just her name on them, and make sure everything else was straight there. Her next stop was the post office to stop her mail for at least a month. She also went by her lawyer's office to sign some forms and let him know that she would be out of town. Dulcie came by later that afternoon to talk with her about house sitting as well. Lillian paid her for the first month up front, and Dulcie seemed quite happy with the arrangement. By the end of the day, Lillian collapsed and went to bed early.

In the next six days, she was so busy that time flew and she slept soundly. Lillian went out with Donovan a couple more times that week, enjoying each date, but trying to keep things where they were, rather than let them progress further. She didn't want to encourage him and then leave for months. She might stay only a month, and then again, she might not come back from Alabama for six months. It was hard to say, and she wanted him to know that was part of the deal of spending time with her for now anyway. The week went swiftly, and she did not have a repeat of the nightmare she had had the day her father was buried. The house began to seem a little less haunted by her father's absence as well, but she wondered if it was just because she knew she would be getting away from it for a while soon.

The day arrived for her to leave, and she got up early, unable to sleep past six. Her flight wasn't until ten. She double-checked her things, and everything was in order. With tears in her eyes, she touched the wall by the front door with fondness, thinking about all the days of laughter that had preceded this one. Donovan swept in the door after that, kissing her and lugging her bags down the steps and into his car. Snow flurries melted on his black hair, and Lillian realized how much she was going to miss him. They drove to the airport hand in hand, not saying much. In the airport, she kissed Donovan chastely on the lips. He pulled her into a big hug and smoothed her hair with his hand.

"Call me when you get there. I want to know that you're safe. Alabama seems like the other side of the world right now." Donovan's green eyes glistened like leaves speckled with morning dew. She felt her own eyes fill up with tears. She hugged him one last time, waving as she walked toward the gate. Once on the plane, the tears streamed freely. Glad she was sitting in a window seat and that the other seat was empty, she cried. She wasn't sure for exactly what, but mainly for her father, partly for leaving Donovan, and perhaps even for herself as she felt a bit lost.

Chapter 3

Perhaps the selfsame song that found a path Through the sad heart of Ruth, when, sick for home
She stood in tears amid the alien corn...
—from "Ode to a Nightingale" by John Keats

Lillian rubbed tired eyes as she stepped off the plane in Montgomery. She collected her checked bags and struggled through the airport. Finally, she made it to the arrivals curbside and looked for the promised black BMW that would ferry her to Magnolian. Her Grand's longtime driver and grounds keeper would be at the wheel. That was a reassuring thought—a familiar face right away. Lillian remembered Percy Jones as a lanky black man with a twinkle in his eyes, a huge smile, and a spring in his step. He had barely changed as he jumped out of the driver's side of the BMW and loped around to meet her. He engulfed her in a big hug, standing back to look at her.

"Miss Lillian! Lord, it's been forever since I seen you. You're all grown up now." He beamed a blinding smile her way as sunlight glinted off a single gold-capped tooth somewhere in his mouth. He didn't look any older than the last time she had seen him.

"Hello, Percy. It's so good to see you." Lillian felt as if her face might shatter from smiling. It was good to see him. He had told her about birds and butterflies the last summer she was here and pointed out the various species—when he wasn't working harder than she had ever seen a man work or crafting little animals in his spare time. She had spent many hours that summer in his old shed, watching him make small creatures out of metal pieces and wood scraps. She still had one of the butterflies he had carved for her on her dresser back home.

They stowed her bags and got in the car. The early morning sunlight shone through a baby-blue sky touched with white wispy clouds. Lillian noted how much warmer it was here—probably about forty-five degrees, where it had been twenty-five in Pittsburgh that morning.

They drove for a few minutes in silence through the city traffic, but Lillian's curiosity made her break the quiet as they hit the outskirts of the city and I-65.

"How's Grand doing these days?' She asked the question innocently, just making conversation.

She was sure she hadn't imagined it. Percy's hands tightened on the wheel.

"She's okay. Doing okay. Just poorly health wise with her heart acting up on her like it is, but everything else is fine." He cleared his throat, not looking at her.

"That's good to hear, Percy. I know you help look out for her." Lillian smiled at him, knowing there was something he wasn't telling her but thinking she would find out later. He probably didn't want to say too much and risk getting into trouble or having what he said repeated.

"I do, and that's a full time job!" He laughed.

She spent the rest of the drive gazing out the window at patches of still green grass and bare or brown needled pine trees as they rolled down I-65. Everything was so flat here—something she had forgotten from her last trip. Lillian knew she would be longing for hills and hardwood trees in a few days, but this landscape had its own charm. She supposed that to those who had lived here for their whole lives, no place looked better. She had felt the same about California for many years, but Pittsburgh had won her heart after just a few months when she saw the first changing of the leaves in fall.

After an hour or so, Percy exited slowly off of I-65 toward

Everwood. He entered a highway and drove some distance in the gathering dusk, passing only a few cars. Daylight ended more quickly here than up North, and soon the sky was royal blue. Lillian could hear the chirp of a cardinal loudly outside the car.

She must have dozed for a bit because the next thing she knew, Percy was gently shaking her shoulder.

"Miss Lillian. We're here." He had come to a stop.

She opened tired eyes and felt the sleep drop away at the sight of the house, Magnolian, built in 1902, as she remembered Grand telling her the last time she was there. The name had come from the trees by the same name that proliferated here in spring. The car was parked at the curve of a long, black-paved, circular driveway. Just two other cars stood in the drive. To the right, Magnolian blazed like someone's childhood gingerbread dream, turreted and iced with frills along its whimsical heights and dips. Its white paint, baby pink trim, and blank gray windows gleamed in the night. It seemed to be inviting her in like an old friend.

Lillian climbed out of the car, stretching like a pent up cat as she smiled.

"Miss Lillian, I'll get the bags. You go on in, all right?" Percy turned to unload the car as she walked, her feet suddenly timid in their steps. The scent of old earth assailed her nose, as did the sound of a lone whippoorwill singing. She shuddered. Someone had once told her that their songs in the night signaled impending death. She reached the wooden steps and stepped on to the porch, seeing the old white swing moving gently in the breeze. She had spent many happy afternoons in that swing reading. She walked on, to the stained-glass panes of the front door. She remembered the door with a jolt with the crying woman's face and a globe of light over her shoulder. Lillian shivered in the dark as she looked into the glass woman's violet eyes, too much like her own for comfort. These were the Granger eyes— passed down to seemingly countless women in the family, or so the legend said. Her grandmother was a Granger before marriage, and this window had been specially commissioned by Butch Stark for his new bride, her great grandmother.

Lillian raised her hand to knock, and the door flew open with a loud groan. Gloom met her eyes. Why had the house looked so cheery at first glance? It certainly didn't now, and the tiny, stern-faced black woman in front of her didn't help matters. Her mouth barely seemed to move as she talked, and her white hair was pulled back severely off of her forehead into a tight little bun at the top of her head.

"Miss Lillian. Your grandmother is upstairs and wishes to see you before bed. She generally goes nowadays around this time." Her tone brooked no argument, and she seemed to have nothing else to say.

Looking at her watch, Lillian moved uncertainly into the foyer—noticing the familiar painting of Alfred Stark hanging against the darkly papered wall—a balding, cheerful-looking paper mill giant who had made the family fortune. To the left, the entrance to the formal dining area stood dark. Only the long shape of a table was visible along with the glinting of light off of china and crystal in the cabinet.

Lillian followed the woman up the staircase. She couldn't remember her name, though her face was familiar. With her unfriendly attitude, the forgetfulness wasn't surprising, Lillian thought. The soft carpet shushed under her footsteps, and a painting of Gretchen Stark Mullins—her mother—hung in the hall. She wore a long yellow dress and stood by a white chair in a garden wild with poppies and goldenrods. Her grin was sly and enigmatic. Lillian would have to ask Grand when it was painted—certainly in the heyday of the garden at Magnolian. She didn't remember the painting from her visit here. The half smile on her lips and her wide violet eyes seemed to follow Lillian up the curved staircase.

They reached the creaky landing with its old wooden flooring, and she remembered her grandmother's room was at the end of the hall. Lillian walked on the slightly creaking dark floor. The wall sconces gave off dim light up here, and it was quiet except for shuffling steps.

It felt as if the house were paused in mid-breath—waiting.

The servant knocked softly on the last door.

"Miz Stark. Lillian's here."

She pushed the door open slowly, and Lillian stepped into her grandmother's room and back in time. She remembered the mahogany everywhere—the king-size sleigh bed with crimson bedspread and pillows of gold, green, and other shades spilling onto the pale, pink-carpeted floor. Her grandmother lay, seeming so much smaller than she remembered, squarely in the middle of the bed. Her hair floated around her like a golden halo cap in the dim light from a Tiffany bedside lamp. Her violet eyes—smaller than the woman's in the painting and Lillian's—looked sunken, and her face was dry and pale. Time had changed the laughing, vibrant woman Lillian had known a few years ago, or was it just late for a tired old woman?

"Grand!" Lillian forgot all hesitation and rushed to her side and gently leaned on the bed, clasping the papery hand she held out to her.

"Lillian, I'm so glad you're here." Grand's voice came out in little more than a whisper. Lillian could see that her first assessment had been correct. She was a feeble woman, her heart problems having taken their toll.

"I know, but I need to let you get your sleep, Grand." Lillian moved to rise and leave, patting her arm, but she gripped Lillian's arm with her hand, hurting her a little.

"No! I'm not tired. Stay with me. I need to talk with you." Her eyes blazed into Lillian's, pools of dusky sky at night. "Leave us, Leticia."

With her command, the maid left, and Lillian pulled a small chair over to her side.

"Sweet Lillian, I am so sorry about your father, but I'm so glad you are here. I only wish it were under other circumstances. We've seen so little of each other in the past few years." Her eyes filled with tears that spilled over and ran into the crevices of her lined face.

Lillian stood from the chair and hugged her gently.

"Don't cry, Grand, it's all right. I am here, and I'll be here for a while." As Lillian spoke, she knew she was telling the truth. Something was bothering her grandmother, and she wasn't going to leave until she got to the bottom of it.

"I just want to tell you to be careful. Don't trust anyone. You can trust me—but no one else." Grand's voice quavered with effort. Her words sounded paranoid—even a little crazy.

"Shh, Grand. It's okay. Whatever it is, we'll fix it." Lillian patted her hand again, wondering if her words were true. They were probably just the words of an overwrought older woman in bad health.

Her eyes closed, and Lillian realized she was snoring gently. She crept out of the room, her feet swishing softly on the plush carpet. She started at finding Leticia waiting in the hall like a silent shadow.

"Your room is on the other end of the hall—last door if you remember." She led her down the hall without a backward glance.

She remembered the room from her stay seven years ago. It was all blond hardwood and light yellow walls with pale ecru carpet. At fifteen, Lillian had called it the sunshine room, she thought with a tired smile. A bedside lamp shed light on the golden bedspread with its mound of ecru, lemon, and white pillows. Her mother's old bookshelf still stood against the wall. On the other wall, by the long window with its sweeping light-yellow brocade curtains, a window reading nook waited for her as it had done on rainy days during her last visit. Lillian felt relieved to be here, and her tiredness overtook her suddenly, making her long for bed.

Leticia backed out of the room on soundless feet, closing the door behind her. Lillian peeled off her clothes, drew back the covers and got ready to hop into bed. She thought better of it, knowing her tendency toward sleepless nights, and walked over to the bookshelf. It had been in the family since the house was built, Grand had once told her. As Lillian reached out to select *Jane Eyre*, she felt a sharp stab on her right heel.

"Ouch. What the—" she looked around, heart pounding and saw a single white leg and claw peeking out from under the ruffled bedspread. Then two green eyes appeared.

"Who are you? You pretty thing!" She was delighted to find a cat in her room—a gorgeous calico, mostly white one at that. The cat allowed Lillian to pet her head before scampering back under the bed. Turning again to the bookshelf, Lillian grabbed *Jane Eyre* and climbed into the high bed. She made it through the first ten pages, and the book fell from her hand as sleep took her.

Sometime during the night, she woke up, shivering. The temperature in the room seemed to have dropped twenty degrees. Utter silence met her ears. For some reason she could not explain, she was afraid to open her eyes. When she did, she saw an outline in the shadows near the dresser. The outline was unsteady, wobbling to and fro like a swathe of bees in sunlight. She rubbed her eyes, her heart beating more quickly. The shadow shimmered into the shape of a man, quivered, and disappeared. She imagined that she heard humming—a familiar tune—but one that she couldn't recall. Where was that sound coming from? Someone outside, or the shadow in the corner? Lillian whimpered and pulled the covers over her head. What had been in the corner? It could have only been a trick of the eyes, but that didn't explain the sudden cold that now seemed to be dissipating. Lillian found herself fiercely longing for Donovan, for the too-silent apple-red house on Fifth Street, and for everything that was familiar.

Chapter 4

Adieu! adieu! thy plaintive anthem fades Past the near meadows, over the still stream...
—from "Ode to a Nightingale" by John Keats

She awoke with what felt like millions of grains of sharp sand in her eyes and a cat on her stomach. Moaning, she rubbed her eyes and crawled out of bed, shifting the cat gently onto the bedspread and scratching her behind the ears. She felt tired, as if she hadn't slept at all. The image of the shadow she had seen and the song she had heard burned behind her eyes. What in the world could it have been? She didn't believe in ghosts, so that idea was pushed out of her mind quickly, but whatever it had been, she didn't want to see it again.

She opened the door on the right side of her room and went to the bathroom, splashing water on her puffy, drawn face. She dug her toothbrush out of her pink suitcase, grinning that she had forgotten to do so last night. Soon enough, she was lipsticked and presentable after a steamy bath with lavender salts in the white claw foot tub.

She got dressed in a lime-green long-sleeved blouse and black leggings, putting on comfortable socks and Mary Janes. Now to face the family—whoever might be downstairs. She expected to see her aunt, but her grandmother might be too weak to make it downstairs this morning.

The scent of bacon, biscuits, and sawmill gravy greeted her as she went down the stairs. In the morning light, everything looked cheerier than it had in the night. She went into the dining room where the mahogany sideboard was laden with food and coffee. Piling her plate high, she grimaced, thinking about how fast ten pounds was going to come on to her petite frame. At just five-foot-three, she had to watch her figure, even though many people assumed she was naturally thin. She sat down at the empty table, wondering who, if anyone, would come in next. She realized that Leticia might be grumpy, but she was a great cook.

Her Aunt Lorelei tottered in on unsteady legs, wearing a muumuu-type dress in dull beige. Lillian was shocked to see her extra bulk after just a few years. Ten years her sister's senior, Lorelei had always been a plumper, meaner shadow of Gretchen. Her ash-blond hair never stood a chance next to Gretchen's titian locks. And of all the Stark women, Lorelei had not inherited the violet eyes most coveted by men for miles around. Her eyes were close-set, dirt-colored pebbles that gave her a hateful look. Perhaps her looks and lack of superior intellect or any outstanding gift had rendered her a target for depression. She had developed it in her early forties, and ten years later, she had only declined, seldom leaving Magnolian, according to Grand when they had talked on the phone.

"Good morning, Aunt Lorelei. How are you?" Lillian smiled at her aunt, not knowing what the response would be. She remembered her as a moody, reclusive woman from the visit seven years ago. She had hardly spent any time with her, though Lillian had made overtures, even as a young girl, and her aunt was not prone to talking much either.

"I'm better than usual. Better than usual," she muttered in a strange, low voice.

Lillian joined her in silent eating for a few moments.

"How do you think Grand is? Will she be coming down for breakfast?" Lillian drank a sip of her coffee, feeling better than she had a few minutes ago.

Food dribbled down Aunt Lorelei's chin as she stared at Lillian. "No, she hasn't come down for breakfast in ages. Leticia takes it to her on a tray. You know Mother, always wanting to be pampered."

Aunt Lorelei cackled, and the sound made the hairs on Lillian's neck rise. She wasn't enjoying talking to Aunt Lorelei, but she had one more question.

"What's the little cat's name I saw last night—the calico?" She smiled at her aunt.

"Oh, that's Renae." Aunt Lorelei looked back down at her plate.

"What a cute name," Lillian said, just glad she knew the creature's name for their next encounter.

She had the sense that Aunt Lorelei wasn't enjoying their conversation much. Lillian decided to finish eating and talk a walk. She could use the fresh air after being cooped up the day before on a plane and in a car. Before she could say anything, her aunt pushed her chair back with a screech and hauled herself up and out of the room, thumping up the stairs.

Shrugging, Lillian headed outside. When she opened the front door and stepped on to the porch, the sound of bird songs greeted her, and she saw a cardinal in the birdbath out front. She hadn't noticed that last night, but it gleamed white in the bright sunlight. Lillian realized soon that though it was fifty-five degrees according to the thermometer near the base of the steps—cool for the South—the humidity was making her blouse sticky. She remembered her father complaining about the heat here, and it brought a smile to her face as she rounded the left side of the house. She was heading for the dirt path that she had walked on so many times before that summer. She had forgotten all about it until now, and she felt her heart leap in her chest with something like happiness. It was just one of several paths behind the house. Her visit to Magnolian was going to do her good. She was sure of it. The fresh air definitely couldn't hurt any. Temperatures were prohibitive in Pennsylvania this time of year—at least for long, leisurely strolls, she thought with a grimace. She planned to hunt out all her old walking haunts here this fall for good exercise and nostalgia.

She found the path only thirty yards from the back of the house. It was shaded and cooler than the open air, and it was only about a yard wide. It felt a bit closed in, but the space was also deliciously secret and small. She shivered a bit as she walked, crunching rocks and underbrush underfoot. Lillian had a strange sense of déjà vu and gasped as she realized it was related to her dream. She laughed aloud nervously. It was just a dream. There were no angry voices or crowds following her as she ran in a filmy night dress. Sunlight glistened on spiderwebs hanging between bushes and small pine trees. Resin filled the air as Lillian went deeper into the woods. She began humming, and then noticed the song she was humming was the one she had heard in her room last night. Shuddering, she clamped her lips shut, determined to walk on. She was about to turn around and head back when she heard a sound that stopped the birds' singing.

Swing low, sweet chariot—

The sound echoed softly through the trees like the sighing of a tired wind. The loveliness of the voice was undeniable. It was the singing of a nightingale in human form. Though in poetry most nightingales were of the female persuasion, this bird was definitely male. Lillian knew that nightingales who sang were male, too. It was only the poets—especially the Romantics like Shelley, Coleridge and Wordsworth—who wanted to believe they were lovelorn females. The thought would have made her smile any other time, but the song made her spine tingle with fear.

Comin' for to carry me home...

The sweet sound was also terrifying and relentless. Lillian clapped her hands over her ears. "Stop. Stop. Stop. This isn't happening." She tried to think. Perhaps it was a man singing—someone working in the woods, but there was no sign of such a man, and the sound was quite close to her. She walked as quickly as she could through the woods back the way she had come toward Magnolian, afraid she would see a shadow. The singing died off to a hum and then silence as she burst out of the woods, gasping at her fast pace. All she wanted to do was get back to the house away from the singer of that song. It was lovely but not human—at least not anymore.

She rounded the house, running and burst through the front door, glad no one was there to see her. She darted up the steps to her room, shutting and locking her door and collapsing on the bed. She closed her eyes for a moment, then opened them, thinking of Donovan. She had forgotten to call him. She took her cell phone out of her purse—thank goodness for nationwide calling plans—and punched in his number. Disappointment and something like relief spread in her chest when he didn't answer. After all, she wanted to talk to him, but what would she say? All is well, but I think I heard a ghost in the woods and saw one last night in my room? The idea was ludicrous. She left a quick message telling him she had arrived safely. Then, feeling a little guilty, she shut off her phone. For some strange reason, he felt worlds away. She didn't want to bring him into all of this. It was her own, just as the man's song was her own. The thought stopped her as soon as it entered her mind. What a strange idea to have, but she knew the singer was a man, maybe in his twenties, and something terrible had happened to him.

Head pounding, Lillian stretched out under the covers and decided to nap. Maybe it was just jet lag, but she felt lethargic as the sun shone through the curtains, signaling approaching noon. She drifted into a dreamless sleep, waking up to a loud pounding on her door.

"Miss Lillian!" The voice was insistent. Leticia was calling. "Your grandmother wants to see you in her room now." Footsteps padded away.

Fully awake now and feeling a little guilty, Lillian went into the bathroom, brushed her hair and applied fresh lipstick. Then she walked down the hall to see Grand. She felt apprehension as she looked at her mother's portrait on the wall as she passed the staircase.

The door was half open when she got there, so she pushed it lightly and walked in. Grand's eyes were closed as she reached her bedside. Lillian wondered if was she having a bad day. The heart trouble had only begun in the last couple years, and Lillian remembered Beverly Stark as a woman who pushed her on the porch swing and played in the Everwood park with her.

"Grand?" She whispered as she pulled up the plush chair next to the bed.

"Yes, dear." To her surprise, Grand's face broke into a big smile. She realized Grand was wearing bright red lipstick and a full face of makeup. She looked much better today than she had last night. Lillian felt a bit relieved. Perhaps Grand's health was better than she thought, or maybe she just had good days and bad days. That was much more likely.

"Did you have a nice morning, dear?" Grand took her hand and smiled, her eyes open and shining now.

"Hmm? Oh, yes. I took a walk on one of the paths behind the house." Lillian swallowed and forced a smile, remembering the ghastly music she had heard.

"Hmm. That sounds nice, dear. Did you enjoy it?" Grand looked at her with something like fear in her eyes as her hands smoothed the blankets on her lap.

"It's lovely back there, Grand. The ferns were so green and full." Lillian looked away from her grandmother's piercing eyes, not knowing why she didn't want to tell her about the man singing and the image in her room last night.

"Well, that's good. I know you'll enjoy all your old places here at Magnolian. I was thinking about them this morning and about walking down the paths with you years ago—only a few times, mind you, but I enjoyed it. I only wish I could still do those things." The old woman sighed in what sounded like relief or exhaustion. "I'd like you to take lunch with me. It's coming in a minute. We have things to talk about." Grand fixed her again with her purplish eyes.

"That sounds wonderful, Grand. What's for lunch?" Lillian smiled.

"Roast beef, potatoes, and squash." Grand arched a light eyebrow. "Aren't those some of your favorites? I seem to remember that."

"Yes, they are." Lillian felt a twinge of pleasure that Grand had remembered for all these years what she liked to eat. Just then the door opened, and Leticia brought in two small trays balanced in each hand. She then brought in hot tea in the silver tea service.

"Rose hip tea—just for you, dear," Grand said with a pat on Lillian's hand. "I hope you like it. If not, we can get something else."

Lillian assured her that she liked the tea, and it was delicious—warm and soothing.

They ate in silence for a few minutes.

"Lillian, I wanted to talk to you before Willoughby Tate gets here." Grand fixed her with a sharp gaze.

"Willoughby Tate? Who's that?" What a name, Lillian thought with a grin she couldn't suppress. He had to be a Southerner.

"Your third cousin on my side. He's whip smart. Don't forget it. He's running his daddy, Joe Tate's, campaign for governor of Alabama. The primary voting is in April. Willoughby's a lawyer, though, here in Everwood. His daddy is, too. Runs in the family, you know." Grand settled back on her bed as Lillian put her tray on the bedside table.

"Oh, I see. Sort of. What's he coming by for?" Lillian looked at her with a furrowed brow.

Grand laughed, and the tinkle rang out in the room like it had once before with a twelve-year-old Lillian. "I asked him to show you around town. What I want to tell you, though, is not to believe anything he or Joe says. Joe's trouble, but he's going to win the election, I guess." Grand took a bite of her oatmeal cookie.

Lillian was puzzled, but she said no more as she sipped her tea and ate another cookie. She put her tray aside on the table thoughtfully.

As she left so Grand could take her usual afternoon nap, Grand's voice stopped her with her hand on the door.

"Don't get tangled up with Willoughby. I'm only inviting him to show you around because he's good at that. He might want to do more, though. He certainly has the reputation for that. He's twenty-seven, never married. Of course, that's not all his fault..." Her voice trailed off, and Lillian realized she was falling asleep. She crept out of the room, wondering what she had meant by it not being his fault. Besides, wasn't twenty-seven the average marriage age these days for men? It was hardly too old or over the hill. Lillian smiled, realizing that her Grand was quite old-fashioned. After all, she had married Jim Stark when she was just eighteen. He had been twenty-four if she recalled her grandmother's stories correctly.

Lillian went back to her room and freshened up before Willoughby was to arrive at an unspecified time. She didn't have anything else to do, and she didn't want to look a mess for some reason. She knew that most Southern women her age prided themselves on their good looks, and they knew how to use them. Her father had always said that about her mother, she thought with a small smile. The pretty calico cat—Renae, she remembered—followed her around the bathroom, tripping her up a few times until she crouched to pet her.

To pass the time, she decided to dig around on the old bookshelf for something to read that she hadn't read in a while. She remembered some old Phyllis A. Whitney novels on there, and one of those would be just the thing to bring back girlhood memories. She saw *The Red Carnelian* at the end of the second row. She didn't remember reading it. She reached up to grab it, and as she did, she saw an old, cracked thin leather volume wedged in beside it, right at the end of the row of books. She grabbed both books, her curiosity piqued by the old book that looked too thin to be a novel.

She laid the Whitney novel at the end of the bed and looked at the thin leather volume. It was a dark brown color and dusty with disuse. The spine opened with a loud crack as she carefully opened the book. She gasped at the first page and at its yellowed edges:

The Journal of Gretchen Leigh Stark

Begun on this date of November 5, 1970—the occasion of my 14th birthday.

How had she never run across this journal before? Then she remembered that she had usually kept to the bottom two shelves of books—the young adult novels or the Jane Austen novels the summer she had been here. On other trips, she had grabbed just one book to read, so this thin volume was probably sitting there for all these years—half hidden, obviously by her mother. She clutched the book to her chest—wanting time to read it. Just then, she heard a loud knock at the front door that reverberated through the house. Somehow she knew that it was Willoughby Tate. Lillian tucked the book back into its former place on the bookshelf with an odd feeling that she didn't want anyone finding it while she was out. She wondered why her mother had left it there and figured it was simple forgetfulness. She smiled, considering it a wonderful turn of fortune. Now she had bedtime reading for the next few weeks.

Chapter 5

Up this green woodland-ride let's softly rove, And list the nightingale she dwells just here.
—from "The Nightingale's Nest" by John Clare

Lillian's first glimpse of Willoughby Tate was from the top of the stairs. He was standing in the foyer, saying something that had Leticia throwing back her head in laughter. She couldn't imagine what would make the dour woman laugh. Perhaps she was only humorless around the women of the house. After noticing that odd occurrence, Lillian was dazzled by the sight of the man who was touching Leticia's arm as he smiled broadly at her. To say that he was a Southern prototype of a gentleman would be an understatement, for he had the towheaded almost silver-laced curly head of hair that most mothers in the Heart of Dixie would swoon over. The sunlight streaming in through the windows played on his hair, setting it on fire like the first sun of morning—palest yellow but white–hot, one would imagine, to the touch. As she slowly walked down the stairs—for she could see she was going to need her composure to stay safe from this man's Apollonian sphere of influence—Lillian noticed the sharp planes and angles of his face with high forehead and pronounced cheekbones. And finally, his eyes—the most arresting shade of blue she had ever seen—not violet but the palest baby blue with yellow flecks in the irises. They reminded her of blue sky reflected in a pool of water, dappled by sunlight. She was close to him now. She took a deep breath to steady her breathing.

"Hello! You must be Lillian. Can I call you Lily?" He took her

hand, turning his brilliant white smile on her. It was almost too much
to take.

"No one's ever called me that before, but sure." Lillian's tongue
felt like a thick wad trapped in her mouth. Knock it off, she angrily
told herself. He's just a charmer like so many other men you've met,
and that had some validity, but she had to admit that she had never
been this close to such a man.

"Shall we go then? Your guide to the delights of Everwood is
here." Willoughby wriggled his eyebrows and swept the door open
with a flourish and a laugh.

They walked out to a late-model silver Mercedes. Lillian had no
idea which model, as such cars were not in her area of expertise, but
she could appreciate the way the paint gleamed in the light.
Willoughby opened the door, and she slid in to the cool leather
upholstered vehicle.

"So, my cousin. We are third cousins, I hear? Are you ready to see
the big town of Everwood? I don't see how it could compare to the
offerings of Pittsburgh—I love your city, by the way, when I go there
on business—but I'll try to make a good show of it." Willoughby
pulled through the circular driveway, going too fast, passing the white
stone pillars that marked Magnolian.

"Yeah, Pittsburgh is pretty great, but I think you have to be a
certain type of person to like it. I'm glad you're the type." She smiled
sideways at him. "Anyway, I can't wait to see Everwood again. I
remember it as charming, but it's been a while." As she talked with
him, she realized that somehow he had put her at ease. Even with his
stunning looks, she felt like she'd known him for years. Just more
evidence that he was a charmer, she thought, smiling inwardly.

"You don't remember me, do you, as studly as I was when you
first ran into me?" He grinned at her as he pulled out onto the main
highway that led into town.

"No, I don't guess I do." That seemed an impossibility, looking at
him now. How could a woman forget a man who looked like this one?

She was puzzled, sifting through memories of past visits. She still came up with nothing.

"Oh, I was a lanky, pimple-faced kid when you would have met me years and years ago. I think you were only eight or so." He grinned, his expensive gold watch flashing in the sunlight.

"Yeah, I'm sad to say I don't remember you at all." Lillian blushed when she realized how that had sounded. Down girl, down, she thought, grinning. She thought about Donovan and felt confused at her quick attraction to Willoughby.

"By the way, since I'm calling you Lily, you can call me Will. I prefer it. My mother chose Willoughby. She is a cousin of your Grand's, you know. All those women liked names of plants and flowers. I used to get teased mercilessly for it. I learned to keep it a secret by going by Will."

"I can do that." She settled back in the seat, enjoying the view. They had driven about two miles down the highway and were approaching town. The sign read Everwood: Population 11455.

"I apologize in advance because this trip is partly political. I'm spending the morning showing you some sights and ordering campaign signs for my dad. We'll swing by his office and meet him. He's a character, and you might remember him." He winked at her.

He pulled into a parking space beside an old forest-green house with white shutters that had a sign in front: Tate & Tate. It was obviously a law office. They got out and walked up creaking steps into a charming space where rooster paintings and ceramic pieces abounded. A secretary sat in the middle of those. She popped bright pink bubble gum and thrust her perky chest out a bit as they walked in. Flipping bottle-blond hair back, she asked, "What can I do for you, Mr. Tate?" Her smile would have felled a lesser man. Willoughby Tate barely seemed to notice it, and she didn't even look at Lillian. Lillian felt an immediate dislike for the woman, and she knew why. She was attracted to Willoughby—Will, she corrected herself—and this woman was as well. Maybe something more was going on between them already.

"I'm just back in for a minute to see my dad. Amber, this is Lily, by the way—my third cousin."

The woman finally smiled at her in a tight grimace. Lillian smiled back, refusing to be pulled into the rivalry.

Lillian felt put off by the cousin label. Amber smiled again acidly at her as they went through an archway to the back of the building. Will knocked on the last door on the left.

"Come in! Come in!" A loud voice boomed.

A florid man was sitting in a huge chair behind a cherry wood desk. A few strands of blond hair glistened off of a balding head. Pale blue eyes like his son's stared out of his fleshy but handsome face. When he stood, his full height must have been nearly six-foot-five unfolded. He, like his son, had presence, but his had been diminished by what looked like hard living and maybe too much alcohol.

"Lillian! I'd know you anywhere, girl. You got the Granger eyes. I haven't seen you in a coon's age." He hugged her and slapped her on the back in the process.

"Hello, Mr. Tate," Lillian said a bit coolly, remembering what Grand had said about this man and his son. His welcome seemed too big somehow, but that was probably just a Southern thing.

"Aw come on, now girl. You know me! Remember when you were five and I dandled you on my knee and gave you a mess of candy when I came out to Magnolian?" His face had a light sheen of sweat that was somehow distasteful.

"You know what? I do. I do. You gave me caramels and Jolly Ranchers! It's all coming back to me now." Lillian did recall him. She also remembered being afraid of the man even then. Something of that fear still stayed with her. His sheer size was intimidating, and he was too brash, too bold for an introvert like her.

"Knock it off, dad. Don't scare her." Will moved to stand beside her. He seemed to sense her hesitance. "I just came to find out about those signs. Are they ready, or do I need to order more? I was going to put a few up on my way back to Magnolian in a while."

"Yessir, they sure are, and I think they look pretty good." They collected about fifty signs reading Joe Tate: The Obvious Choice for Guv, and they were on their way, Amber snapping gum and waving as they left.

"Don't mind my dad. He's a little overbearing, but he means well." Will frowned, as if he weren't sure of this claim himself, as they stepped out the door and headed down the steps to the car.

"Let's head to Lulu's for lunch. They have great catfish and collard greens." He opened her car door and let her in, jogging around to his side to get in.

They had a lovely lunch at the small diner with its cheerful pink and white décor. Will regaled her with local stories of flooding thirty years ago as well as history and gossip. Lillian realized she was totally at ease with him. Myriad locals came up to pump Will's hand, and the gamut of women—Mary Lou, Louise, Laura Lynn, and Scarlett—came by to flirt and ask him how things were going. More than one jealous look came her way. She got the distinct impression that Will had dated or bedded at least half of the women who did come by. That thought made her feel uncomfortable and inexperienced.

"So, are all those women your exes?" She asked, wanting to know but afraid to find out at the same time. She ate a bite of her turnip greens, looking down at her plate.

"Ha. You must think I'm a total player. Only three of them." He winked at her. "Amber was my latest girlfriend. It didn't work out, but that's why she was shooting daggers at you this morning." He shrugged.

Lillian recoiled inwardly at this revelation. If Will's type of woman was Amber, she didn't stand a chance. She didn't stand a chance anyway, she thought to herself angrily. She needed to cut her schoolgirl fantasies off right there. She was only setting herself up for disappointment with a guy as handsome as Will.

They ate in silence for a few more minutes. The statement about Amber hung between them uncomfortably. She regretted bringing up all the other women who flirted with him. It made it sound like she cared one way or the other.

"That was delicious. That blackberry cobbler was like nothing I've ever eaten." Lillian smiled as they headed out of the restaurant and walked out onto Main Street in the middle of town. The historic brick buildings and the railroad track made for a picturesque scene. A railroad mural on a building across the street pointed to some of the history of Everwood. Ladies who lunch swirled past like colorful butterflies even in autumn as they headed to the small boutiques, restaurants, and antique shops along the street.

"I love this street. It's so vibrant, especially for a small town," Lillian remarked as they got to the car.

"I agree with you there. Everwood has put a lot of work into revitalization where a lot of other small towns around the country are dying. I think this one is actually improving." He smiled and held the car door open for her.

They got into the car and he said, "Maybe tomorrow we can go by the historical society. I need to get some of these signs out today before I head back to work. What do you think?" Will looked at his watch and grinned at her.

"Sounds like a plan," she said, trying to be nonchalant. The truth was, she would love to spend more time with Will.

They drove back out toward Magnolian, pulling the car over sporadically to place a sign in a friendly voter's yard or business lawn. Lillian hid a few snickers behind her palm when the women who owned the houses or businesses ran out after seeing Will in the front yard. There was no denying he was a favorite with the Everwood ladies. She guessed every town had at least one coveted hunk, though.

Their last stop was a dirt road turnoff on the right side of the highway, but Will drove down it, rather than getting out and placing a sign. Lillian was puzzled.

"Who lives out here? Aren't we close to Magnolian?" She glanced down the road and didn't see a house, only a water tower.

"I know," he said, putting his hands out on the wheel as they pulled to a stop. I didn't tell you about this stop. This is one of my favorite old haunts in Everwood. The old water tower. It's just a quarter mile from Magnolian. There's a path that goes from here to there, in fact, if you want to walk it."

Will parked, and they got out. A breeze was blowing, and pine trees and bushes surrounded them. Looming in the middle of the woods was a white, battered water tower. Lillian realized she had not been down this Magnolian path before and felt a thrill of pleasure at another path to travel during her daily walks. It was somehow all the more thrilling that Will Tate had been the one to bring her here.

"I bet you've brought a lot of girls out here. I've been down some of the Magnolian paths, but I missed this one somehow." They got out of the car, and she smiled over the hood at him.

He smiled back at her. "You might be on to something there about the girls, but all joking aside, I come here alone—usually when I have something major to think through. Sometimes I come before a killer trial. I've done some of my best thinking here. My father showed it to me when I was a young boy." Something about his father knowing about this path seemed strange, but she didn't mention it.

The breeze blew and whipped leaves around their ankles as they walked through the area around the tower. Will clasped her hand, holding it as they approached a small path to the left. Leaves and pine needles crunched under their feet. His hand and hers felt natural together, but she was taken aback by his advance. She would never have expected it from him—not after seeing all the women he could be spending time with.

"I've been wanting to do this all day," he said and leaned toward her at the head of the dark path, kissing her. Warmth spread through her as he put his arms around her and pulled her closer. She could feel the softness of his green polo shirt and the hardness of his muscular arms against her hands. She broke the embrace, stumbling back a bit and laughed nervously, but she didn't let go of his hand.

"I'm sorry. I know that was crazy." Will smiled and raked a hand through his golden curls. Still holding hands, they walked down the path. The trees closed in on them and made it appear that evening was approaching. Wind whistled through the trees, but no birds chirped. The silence was heavy, and a few steps more down the path and Lillian wanted to head back to the car. Her heart was pounding erratically. She was frightened, but she didn't know why. Will seemed unaffected, but she could hardly breathe. She felt a palpable presence that stood apart from her and the man with her.

He stopped in the path and drew her to him again, kissing her fiercely. Her heart racing, she broke away and ran back to the head of the path, gulping air as she burst back out into sunlight and birdsong.

"What the hell was that all about?" Will clenched his fists angrily at his side and stalked back to the car. So, the golden boy wasn't so golden when he didn't get what he wanted, she thought. He had brought her out her to seduce her, laughable as the thought was when he could have any woman he wanted in Everwood. She felt anger and longing simultaneously. She also wondered if he had felt what she had on the path—that pressing presence. She couldn't wait to get out of here.

They climbed into the car in silence, and he backed down the path, jerkily and too fast.

"I'm sorry. I just—it doesn't feel right back there." Lillian murmured, feeling defensive and angry.

"Oh, okay. Yeah, I think I know what the problem is." He gave her a long, measured stare. "Are you a virgin?" He looked into her eyes, and the yellow flecks danced with malice. He enjoyed making her squirm.

They had reached Magnolian and were driving through the white pillars down the drive.

"Let me out now. Thanks for the tour." Lillian jerked the car door open and marched to the house, panting in fury. Despite her anger, she was proud of herself for not cowering or simpering in the face of Will's rudeness.

She heard the other door slam.

"Wait! Lily. I'm sorry," he said as she climbed the steps to the front door and reached the porch.

"Save it for Amber or whoever needs it. Have a nice afternoon." She opened the door and slammed it shut, knowing he wouldn't follow her. He didn't. She stood by the door, heart thudding, and heard his car pull away.

She trudged heavy hearted up the steps, tears pooling in her eyes after the fact. Grand was right. Will was not to be trusted, nor was his father.

When she got to her room, she remembered her phone had been off for a while. She turned it back on and admitted to herself that she missed Donovan. The phone pinged, and she saw one text message from him that simply read *I'm glad you're safe. I miss you. Call me any time.* What a different response from that of Will just minutes ago, she thought with happiness. She would call him after she had read some more in her mother's journal.

Slipping the journal out of its nook on the bookshelf, she lay back on her bed and relaxed. The first few entries were normal ones for a spirited fourteen-year-old girl—parties, groans about parents. Then she came across one that startled her, written some months later. She realized that it would have been a year in to the journal. The first year only had about ten entries:

November 15, 1971

I saw him again. He was clear cutting some brush behind Magnolian. He has a noble forehead as Jane Austen would put it, and his smile. I tried not to pay him much attention. I didn't want mother to notice.

Lillian's brow furrowed. Who in the world could she mean? She realized she had been reading for an hour and that it was time for dinner. Six o'clock sharp without fail, Grand would be ready for it to be served, Leticia had said. Lillian secreted the journal away again and heading downstairs. She looked at her mother's portrait in the hall wondering one thing. What secrets did you have, Mother?

Chapter 6

Hush! let the wood-gate softly clap, for fear The noise might drive her from her home of love...
—from "The Nightingale's Nest" by John Clare

Dinner was an awkward affair, even though Lillian was glad to see Grand looking flushed and happy at the dinner table, her golden hair coiffed to perfection. Joe Tate was sitting at the table when Lillian got downstairs. Aunt Lorelei hobbled in wearing the most outrageous shade of orange that made her look like an overstuffed Halloween pumpkin. She grinned at Joe with obvious pleasure and ignored the rest of the table, pointedly.

"Darling," Grand smiled warmly across the table at Lillian. "I've invited Joe for dinner this evening, and Will is on the way as well." Joe grinned at her from across the table.

Lillian sat down, hoping no one noticed her flaming cheeks. She didn't know if she could stand dinner with Will, knowing he was laughing at her inside, having guessed correctly, if meanly, about her lack of experience. The truth was that the lack of experience wasn't what had driven her out of his arms this afternoon. It had been the feeling she had had in the woods. She shivered, recalling it.

When Will walked in, she didn't meet his eyes. He sat down two seats from her.

"Hello again, Lily." He locked eyes with her, not looking away.

"Hi," she answered with clipped tones as she speared a piece of creamy chicken. She wasn't going to give this man the time of day after what he had said to her. She didn't care if he was a third cousin.

Who paid attention to those anyway?

Joe Tate made bawdy jokes and laughed uproariously through much of dinner. Grand humored him, as did Will. Aunt Lorelei made eyes at him all evening, and it struck Lillian then that she was in love with Joe Tate. Lillian wondered for how long and if it had anything to do with her aunt's single status after all these years. Maybe she had pined away for Joe for decades. The thought brought a smile to Lillian's face and made her feel a little better at Will's expense. Joe seemed more irritated with her aunt's attentions than anything. Lillian knew he was married, so this made sense. Lillian was more or less silent, only speaking when spoken to.

"So, Lillian," Joe boomed, "how long are you staying here? What are your plans while you're here?"

"I'm not sure how long I'll be here. I plan to take a few courses at the community college—maybe a winter term course and go from there or just get a job or an internship. I'm kind of open about the future, obviously." She ate a spoonful of buttery brown rice.

"Sounds like a good plan, young lady. I always like to hear from young people who have goals. That's what our state needs now more than ever. I hope you're around long enough to help with my gubernatorial campaign. It's kickin' into high gear here in about a month. The primary is in April, you know." He grinned at Lillian, but there was something she didn't like in that look. It was almost a challenge of some sort, but she didn't know for what. Could Will have told him about what had happened this afternoon? The thought of that made her cheeks flame.

"I helped a little today already with some signs," she said archly, fixing Will with a look that could have killed.

Will laughed softly, dipping his chin, and had the decency not to say anything else as Grand and Joe looked at Will and Lillian questioningly. Soon the talk moved on to other things: what the dirty Democrats were up to in the local elections coming up—apparently everyone in Everwood that counted, anyway, was a Republican—the high price of milk, and the new YMCA that was going up in town. Lillian yawned after coffee and dessert and pushed back her chair, ready to escape.

"I've had a long day. I think I'm going to have a quiet evening and turn in, if you'll excuse me." She was planning to call Donovan and read her mother's journal. Those two activities were highly preferable to sitting at the table a moment longer.

"Lily, wait. Can we take a turn around the house? It's practically balmy out tonight." Will looked at her with pleading in his blue eyes and smiled.

She sighed. "Okay, let's go." She rose quickly from the table, wanting to get this over with. What could he possibly have to say to her that was worth hearing?

Joe, Grand, and Aunt Lorelei looked at them both with puzzlement and then resumed conversation as Leticia came in to start clearing plates off of the table.

The night air was cool with no trace of humidity—often a rarity even in autumn in Alabama. The stars winked like so many pinprick lights on a backdrop. Lillian took a deep breath, wondering what Will was going to say as they stepped off the porch onto the grass beside the driveway. She certainly wouldn't be the first to speak.

"There's no good way to say this, but I'm sorry. I'm really sorry for what I said, for what I asked you. There's no excuse for it." Will stood with his hands in his jeans pockets, looking at her as they strolled across the front lawn.

"Apology accepted, but why did you say it? Did you really think I was going to sleep with you on the path or under the water tower?" In spite of herself, Lillian smiled a little.

"Well, sort of. I mean, no. I mean—let me explain. This isn't an excuse. It's just what's been going on with me for the last six months." Will took a deep breath, and Lillian saw pain etched in his features. It was hard not to listen to him sympathetically.

"I was engaged to a wonderful woman—a teacher here in town.

Her name was Tansy Pace. She and I—I thought—were very happy together, perfect match and all that. She was gorgeous and the kindest woman I've ever known—maybe barring you so far." He smiled briefly. Then the lines of tension settled back into his face. Lillian realized that his jocular manner was simply a cover for stronger, darker emotions.

"Anyway, to make a long story short, we were to be married December 1st—just a few weeks from now, you know. So, one night, I got a call. Her mother was hysterical. She had called a few times that night—I was still at the office and we had no plans for that Tuesday night, but they did. Her mother couldn't get her on the phone, so she finally drove over to Tansy's house." His voice broke, and Lillian touched his shoulder as she saw tears glinting in his eyes in the starlight.

"She walked into the bathroom after calling for Tansy all over the house. She found her dead in the tub. She had taken a bunch of pills and killed herself. I still can't believe she did it or that she did it then knowing her mother would be the one to find her. It was so cruel. She must have been out of her mind because she was never cruel to me." Will cleared his throat noisily.

Lillian touched his arm. "But why? Why would she do that?" How could any woman do that, she wondered, especially a woman who had been engaged to a man like Will? Lillian stopped her line of thinking short. Just because he looks like an angel certainly doesn't mean he is one, she told herself firmly. She knew that all too well after his stunt on the path earlier.

"Oh, that's easy. It was because of me. I'd been flirting with Amber every day in the office, and she could see it when she came by to meet me for lunch or when she just dropped in to say hi. I think she realized or thought that she'd made a terrible mistake—that I could not love her like she needed to be loved, and she thought that time was running out on all her dreams. She'd been hurt before over and over. I swear, though, that nothing happened—then—between Amber and me. That only happened after her death when I needed consolation." His face hardened. "So, I guess I did just the thing she feared, and I've been on a crash course for months now. Amber was my plaything—just something to soothe the pain for about a month after. The crazy thing is that she's not even mad at me. I dumped her, and she would still do anything I asked." He snorted but then frowned again.

The thought of Amber doing anything he asked was not appealing, and she tried to shift her mind off of the image.

"So, what does all this have to do with me? By the way, I didn't run from you because I'm inexperienced. I ran because I felt something out there in the woods. I had to get away." She clasped her arms in the moonlight, hugging herself and trembling at the thought of it. Her head swirled, trying to figure out how she should feel about Will after his revelations. She felt sympathy but also anger that he had treated Amber and himself that way.

"You felt something? Really? I believe you because you look like you've seen a ghost just thinking about it." He meant his words in jest, but they made her think of what had been happening to her since her father's death, the nightmares and shadowy men and singing ghosts. "I'm so sorry, Lily. And don't you know what this all has to do with you?"

He turned to her, facing her straight on, and clasped her hands in his. "You're the first woman who has made me feel anything real since Tansy died. It scared me. I thought I'd prove you were like all the rest—fine with a one-night stand and not caring if it went further. I was trying to push you away. I'm sorry, but that's why I acted like I did. I'm a jerk." He looked down at the ground as they walked and then stopped again. He gathered her in his arms, and she could feel his heart beating like a metronome as he smoothed her hair. "Can you forgive me, Lily? I mean, really forgive me?" The emotion in his voice wiped out any other possibilities.

"Of course I can forgive you. You've been under tremendous

stress." She stepped out of his embrace. "But I don't want more than friendship from you—at least not now. You need to heal, and I'm willing to be a friend to you if you need someone to talk to or whatever." She swallowed, not sure if she wanted that or more, but knowing it was the only answer at this point.

"I can respect that. You'd be crazy to take up with me right now. I'm a mess." He laughed nervously, pushing back blond curls.

"Honestly, Will, I have a lot of sorting out to do myself. Now, let's go in. All is forgiven. We start fresh today." She took his arm and walked him back toward the house.

He stopped , putting his hands on his head. "What an idiot I am! I remember Grand telling me why you were here—your father's death and just getting some space from everything to think. I'm even sorrier for what I did, and I'm sorry for your loss. Can I at least try to make it up to you by taking you to the historical society tomorrow? I think you'd like it." He stopped in front of the sorrowful stained glass front door, his down turned mouth mirroring that of the woman in the pane for an eerie moment.

"Of course. What time is good for you? You're the working man." She punched his arm playfully, and he smiled tentatively at her.

"How about ten? They'll be open then, and we can grab a burger afterward at Pine's. Best burgers within a hundred miles." He smiled, and the lines that she had seen disappeared from his face.

"It's a date." She grinned in earnest for the first time that night.

"Until tomorrow, then." He blew her a playful kiss as he sauntered down the driveway toward the Mercedes. His ego seemed no worse for the wear after his confessions, Lillian thought with a wry grin. She watched him drive away and then went back inside, bypassing the sitting room and heading upstairs. She was emotionally wrung out after hearing the tragic story of Tansy, and poor Will. She couldn't imagine the pain of that. Men flirted with other women all the time, but their fiancés didn't kill themselves over it. Obviously, Tansy had had other problems.

Changing into a flannel set of pajamas and getting ready for bed, she decided to call Donovan Ross first since it was 9:00 p.m. his time on the East Coast, and she knew he had classes and private piano lessons on Tuesdays. The phone rang seven times and went to his voice mail. Swallowing a lump of disappointment, Lillian left a voice mail on his phone, telling him she missed him and hoped they could catch each other soon. It had only been two days, and she realized it felt like two weeks. Her phone beeped with a message. It was Dulcie reporting that all was well with the house and the car and telling her to have a great trip. That was a relief—one less thing to worry about while she was away.

Lillian got up and slipped Gretchen's journal out of its slot, feeling a frisson of excitement go through her. The next few entries in November were disappointing—just news about the local school and Thanksgiving plans. The interesting thing was that the number of entries had gone up—four already in November where the last year had only held a few more than that. It seemed the young Gretchen had had a lot to confide in her journal.

December 1st marked another intriguing entry:

I was outside helping Lorelei with the raking after school when I heard the most gorgeous singing. It was him of course; I have decided he sounds like a nightingale. He's also dark like one and mysterious. He smiled at me last week, but I rarely see him. His father Percy keeps him quite busy, and today he was gathering wood in the woods behind our house.

Lillian shivered after reading those lines. She had heard that nightingale singing. Thoughts assailed her furiously. It sounded like the young man was Percy's son and that her mother had been in love with him or at least that he had been her first crush. That would mean—that would mean that her young man had been black or at least biracial, Lillian thought. No big deal nowadays in some places, but a big deal here in the 70s and still a big deal here from what she knew. It wouldn't have mattered to a headstrong girl, though. Gretchen had been fifteen, after all. Crushes happen, but they don't necessarily turn into more. But what if this one had? The question popped into Lillian's head and she gasped. Something about the thought gripped her and would not let go. The 1970s, even after Civil Rights, was not a good time to challenge long-held Southern thought on the matter. What if her mother had done so? Surely not. She had been happily married to John Mullins. Certainly, if she was the love of her father's life, then the love of Gretchen's life must have been John. Right? The thought niggled at Lillian's brain. She realized that she knew very little of her mother's life before in Alabama, and that her father could no longer tell her—even if he had known about her mother's past. She also thought of his vehement reactions to Southern racism and shivered. She would get some answers tomorrow. Who was this young man, and what had he meant to her mother? Why was he singing in the woods, even now, unless he was alive and living out there somewhere? She knew that idea was silly. Feeling she could read no further tonight, she decided to go to bed early.

She lay tossing and turning for a half hour, hearing creaks and the thumping of insects at the window and pine cones on the roof. Finally, she drifted off to sleep. The dream came to her again, and she realized that the woman running in the forest on the path was not her. It was her mother, Gretchen Stark, as a young woman—maybe age sixteen. Her father's face floated above with its worry, but no words came from his mouth. He just stared at Gretchen in great sorrow. The angry voices were closer now, and Lillian realized there were just two of them. Suddenly, in the midst of her mother's running, which Lillian could feel—the dirt under bare feet and the sharpness of rocks—a haunting song rang out, full of longing and tenderness.

Swing low...

The words were hummed and sung intermittently as her mother ran on. Lillian wrenched herself awake, shivering in the extreme cold of the room. Her fingers, gripping the covers, felt like icicles. As she opened her eyes, they were drawn to a shadow against the wall near her dresser. The outline was more vivid tonight and was that of a man—a tall, handsome man with mocha-colored skin. He held up a hand as if beseeching or wanting something. Lillian screamed, and he disintegrated.

Thumping feet sounded in the hall a minute later, and Aunt Lorelei banged on the door.

"Lillian. Lillian! Are you okay? What's going on?" Her voice was insistent.

"I'm fine. I'm okay—just a nightmare," Lillian gasped as her aunt opened the door hastily and walked up to the bed, purple nightgown flapping around her. She looked wide awake, and Lillian wondered if she had even been sleeping. She had come quite quickly in response to her screaming.

"Oh. Are you prone to nightmares then?" Lillian noticed her aunt's narrowed eyes, looking at her speculatively in the shadow-filled room.

"No, never—really. I'm fine. Really. I'll be back to sleep in no time." Lillian smiled in what she hoped was a convincing way as her aunt sniffed.

"Well, nobody but your mother ever had any trouble in this room. She had bad dreams, too, and used to wake up crying in the night. I'd come in and comfort her sometimes. Sometimes, I'd just listen to her wail." The memories seemed to trouble her aunt.

Lillian stayed silent, not asking what she wanted to about Percy's son. She would read on in the journal or talk with Grand later. She sensed a strange emotion in her aunt that she could not readily name—something like jealousy. In the wee hours of the morning, it scared her a little.

"All right. I can see you don't want to talk about it. Suit yourself. At least try to get some sleep." Her aunt stalked out of the room, wobbling as she walked.

Lillian breathed a sigh of relief as she left. In minutes, she was asleep again, and no shadows or dreams interrupted her night.

Chapter 7

Laughing and creeping through the mossy rails here have I hunted
like a very boy,
Creeping on hands and knees through matted thorn To find her nest,
and see her feed her young.
—from "The Nightingale's Nest" by John Clare

Lillian rose early, got her shower, enjoying the hot spray, and hurriedly put some makeup on. She chose a peach sweater and tan slacks to wear along with warm brown suede boots that had been a gift from her father last Christmas. She wanted to read a journal entry or two before breakfast. The smell of grits and eggs wafted up from the dining room already. Lillian looked at her watch: 8:15 a.m. That gave her a few minutes to read before Will got there.

Eagerly opening the journal to the next entry on December 4th, she found an interesting description of the family's trip to find a Christmas tree, but nothing about Percy's son. Then on December 10th, she found another entry.

I have been going to the garden after dinner most evenings, hoping to run into S. He works here all day, but I'm in school so long that I rarely get to see him, though I think about him constantly. I wonder if he really notices me when we pass each other. After all, he is almost eighteen—just out of school last May. I must seem young to him. Tonight, I caught a glimpse of him and was going to talk to him about the rose beds for next year—as a topic of conversation before he moved on to his next chore and went to back to the house down the road—but Lorelei walked outside just then, and I had to ignore him. She is cruel and full of jealousy since she is so ugly and mean, and if she suspected my feelings for him... I keep this journal under lock and key for that reason. I wish she would leave home, but I fear she will never marry! Instead, she just pines over Joe Tate, who is nearly twice her age and married.

So the vibes she had gotten from Aunt Lorelei at dinner had been correct. She was in love with Joe Tate and had been for years. She would have been about twenty-three when this entry was written.

Intriguingly, the journal skipped six months as if nothing of consequence had happened. June 15th, 1973, was the next entry and the last one she had time to read at the moment:

Joe Tate came by tonight. He's so infuriating with all his talk of "the niggers are doing this and the niggers are taking over that." I hope he doesn't win the mayoral race. I'm almost sure he's one of the men in town who still wears a white hood. Life has been rather mundane for me of late. I've only caught glimpses of S., but he smiles just at me each time—even when my sister or other people are around. I don't think anyone has noticed, but I have. I wonder how I could have time to talk with him alone. I'm thinking about it...

Lillian closed the journal reluctantly, running her fingers over the aged spine before slipping the book into its hiding place. She needed to get down to breakfast. Will would be picking her up soon enough.

She was alone at the breakfast table and was a bit disappointed, having hoped she could talk with Grand about the journal today. She was not sure about the shadow in her room or the singing and didn't plan to mention it. She ate her grits and eggs and drank a hot cup of coffee. An idea came to her as she ate. If she could find Percy around outside before Will came to pick her up, she could broach the subject of his grandson, somehow, delicately. She wouldn't mention her mother. She just wanted to see what he would say about his grandson. Would he tell her he was alive and happy somewhere far away? In a way, she hoped so, but in another way, she knew that news would just be more confusing for her at this point.

She finished her food quickly and went out the front door. As luck would have it, Percy was treating ant beds in the front yard some distance away. She walked over to him, thinking about what she would say when she got there.

"Hi, Percy. How's the ant mission going?" She smiled at him, rubbing her hands together.

He pulled his white mask down and grinned. "Well, they keep trying to hang on, but I just about got them. Something you need, Miss Lillian?" He poked at the ant bed again with the sprayer.

"Oh, I was just thinking about how you had lived generations with this family and always have cared about me and my family. I was curious about yours. I know you're older than Grand, but you hide it well. I wondered, how many children do you have?" She felt low asking about something she cared little about apart from the ghostly singing and journal entries, but she felt a sense of urgency. She needed to know more about S. and about what had been happening to her.

His dark face blanched a bit—noticeably. "Well, lessee. We got five children: Ava, Percy III, but we call him Trip, John, Lewis, and Mary. Now I got eight grandchildren already, too and one great grandchild. I'm so proud of them all." He smiled, but he seemed to be guarding his words.

"Oh, I see. That's wonderful, Percy. Do they all live around here still?" She dug her toe into the dirt at her feet, looking at the ground.

"Nah, just two of them. The rest lit off for elsewhere—trying to make a better life." His mouth turned down, thinking about this, but then he smiled. "You know, I really appreciate you asking, and you know I love you and yours like my own, so I guess I got a mess of kids, grands, and great grands." He went back to spraying ants, and

Lillian took it as a signal that the conversation was over.

"I know you treat us and care for us like your own. I'm glad your family is all well, too. Thanks for everything, Percy. See you later. Good luck with the ants."

Lillian walked slowly across the yard, dead pine needles crunching under her boots, lost in thought. Percy had another son with a name that started with an S. Unless the S was a middle initial, but she didn't think so. The young Gretchen seemed simple, and S would certainly be her true love's first initial. So, the question was why Percy would deny his existence. What could be so bad that he wanted to forget him or his life before others? Smiling despite her troubled mind, she met Will as he swung his car into the drive in front of her. She jumped into the car, ready to get away from Magnolian for a few hours.

She began talking as soon as she was in the car, her words falling over each other. "Can we head to the historical society first?" She tried to keep the eagerness from her voice, but Will must have heard it. He looked at her with one eyebrow raised.

"My, my, my. I never pegged you for a history buff. I'd heard you were a bookworm, though. I guess you just never know. Of course we can go there first. I live only to serve you, miss." He bowed his head jokingly and shifted the car into drive, passing smoothly through the moss-speckled posts to exit Magnolian. Lillian felt her spirits lift as they drove through the pillars. The dreams and other things that had been going on made Magnolian feel oppressive. She had just gotten here but was glad to be leaving daily to do other stuff.

"Great. Thanks. I just want to do a little research, that's all. Everwood is a fascinating place, you know." Lillian's excitement was rising. She wiped her sweaty palms on her pants. If something had happened to S., surely the local news would have covered it. Those archives would be in the Everwood Historical Society's collection, she was sure. If they weren't there, the local library would have them, but often groups like these joined forces.

Will laughed as if he were very amused. "Sure it is. Tons of excitement going on here. Try to contain yourself when you read about the Great Flood of '69." They drove along Main Street as stray leaves skittered across the road along with the odd brown squirrel. He pulled into a short driveway attached to a Melba peach old house with white shutters. The swinging sign identified it as the Everwood Historical Society.

They got out of the car. Lillian breathed in the bracing fall air on the way to the door.

"One plus of this place is that you'll love Miz Fanny. She's great and can help you with anything you need. She should be in today, though she works part time these days." He held the creaky door open as a little bell tinkled, announcing their arrival.

The scent of roses, emanating from a big-breasted woman who came from the back of the room with dozens of chinking gold bracelets on, enveloped Lillian. Her dramatic eye makeup and puffy auburn hair barely caught the eye at all compared to her shocking-yellow tiered, ruffled dress.

"Come in! Come in, Will. And you are?" She had her manicured hand on Lillian's back and looked at her closely.

"I'm Lillian Mullins. Beverly Stark's granddaughter." Lillian felt a bit nervous as Miz Fanny sized her up with leonine eyes.

"Well, of course you are! I'd recognize those violet eyes anywhere, honey. You here just to look around, or you have something you want to find out?" She looked at Lillian seriously.

"I have some research I'd like to do. I'd appreciate any help with finding things," Lillian answered with a smile, liking Fanny immediately.

"Okay, in that case, let me show you around the place, and you can dig in. I'll be glad to help as you need me." She swept them first to the corner where computers with were set up. In the back, countless newspapers and microfiche readers for the others that weren't stocked were kept. To the left, historical knickknacks from the area gleamed in glass cases.

"If you need anything, just holler. I'll be in and out of the back. I got some new stuff in today and need to reorganize things, but I'm here to help." She floated away on a cloud of fresh roses.

Will chuckled. "She's great, isn't she? I can tell by your face that you agree."

Lillian agreed and then headed for the newspapers. She knew she was looking for something in the early 1970s, and she figured she only had a little time today before Will would get antsy. She also didn't want him looking over her shoulder, so she needed to be quick. To her surprise, he told her he would be on the computers. He had a project to work on for his father's campaign. That suited her just fine and bought her some time.

She went through the 1972 papers, beginning in June. She found nothing but interesting tidbits and hairstyles from the 1970s along with mentions of Joe Tate as the new mayor. She was grateful that the town's paper in those days—news wise—had only been a few pages long. In the 1973 batch, the December 10th issue of *The Everwood Edition,* she hit pay dirt. The article was titled, "Missing Local Young Man's Disappearance Mystifies Authorities." The name that had caught her eye in the second line of the article was Samson Jones. She took a deep breath and called Fanny over to get the article printed. Feeling she could trust Fanny, she asked tentatively, "Were you here in Everwood when he disappeared? I mean, did you know him?"

"Who? Samson? Oh, sure. I grew up with him. We went to school together after desegregation you know. He was a good kid—handsome and smart and a great singer. He used to sing in the halls at school every day. People called him the Nightingale. There was some said nasty things about him when he disappeared, but many of us missed him greatly and still think about him when we hear birds singing like he did." Lillian was touched to see that Fanny's golden eyes had grown misty with remembering. She had started when Fanny referred to Samson—for she now was sure of his name—as a nightingale, since she had thought of him that way as well—as a nightingale in death. She tried to keep her face straight as Fanny went on.

"He was real sweet, too. It was the craziest thing. He was out at Magnolian one day, and then he wasn't. The family was real torn up about it—his family and the Starks, I mean. Your grandfather spent all the time and money he could spare looking for a trace of him. None was found. His daddy, Percy, took it so hard, it was like he forgot he'd ever lived. He never mentions the boy anymore. I think it hurt him real bad." Fanny handed her the printouts as Will walked up.

"Found something, huh?" he asked, grinning and looking at his watch.

"Yes," Lillian said shortly without explaining. She couldn't wait to get back home to read the article and think about things, but she knew lunch with Will was required first. It wasn't that it was a burden, she thought with a grin. She just had other things right now that trumped even being with a great-looking man like Will.

They drove over to Pine's for burgers. The homey decor with Everwood pictures from years gone by and old signs and posters as well as the friendly staff made it a joy. Once again, Lillian noticed all the female eyes on Will. One woman, Monica, seemed to catch his attention. He told Lillian she was a lawyer in town, too.

"Oh yeah? It sounds like a match made in heaven." Lillian popped a fry into her mouth and smirked at him.

He pursed his lips, "Um, probably not. Lawyers fight too much as it is. Think of them married to each other." He laughed and took a bite of his burger. The rest of lunch went pleasantly by, and Lillian was able to forget the article for an hour.

On the drive home, though, the anticipation was building to read it. She barely looked at the lovely old restored homes and businesses as they went back down Main Street.

"What is it with you today? You're as nervous as a jackrabbit. I'm the one who has to argue before the judge today to get a scum bucket off the hook, and I'm as cool as a cucumber. What's up?" Will lifted his hands playfully from the wheel to show his dry armpits. She smacked him lightly as he turned into Magnolian.

"I'm fine—just not sleeping well lately. That's all." She wasn't ready to confide anything about the journal or the ghost to Will. She couldn't even believe in the ghost herself yet, but she knew the article she held was proof that something had happened at Magnolian— something that still haunted the place, or at least her.

"If you say so. You sure seem interested in whatever you found at the historical society, but I won't pry. For now anyway." He smiled at her leeringly. "I'll call you. I have to run—work to do. He pecked her on the cheek, and she got out and ran lightly up the steps and into the house. She smacked headlong into Aunt Lorelei and wondered if she had been spying out the window on them. The article in her hands fluttered to the ground. She quickly snatched it up off the floor, but not before her aunt had gotten a look at it, she was sure.

"Excuse me, Aunt Lorelei. I'm sorry. I was in a rush." Lillian moved away from her, keeping the article out of her reach.

"I'm fine. Just watch out next time." Dark eyes darted toward Lillian, and a look of knowing crossed Lorelei's face. She turned with a flounce of black tent dress and walked into the living room. Lillian heard the television flip on. Unsettled, she climbed the stairs to her room.

Chapter 8

Lost in a wilderness of listening leaves, Rich Ecstasy would pour its luscious strain, Till envy spurred the emulating thrush To start less wild and scarce inferior songs...
—from "The Nightingale's Nest" by John Clare

Lillian locked her door and sat on the bed, digging a pen and some paper out of the nightstand. Both looked like they had been around since her mother's childhood, and they probably had, but they would do. She couldn't see dragging her laptop out of her carry-on bag, since she hadn't used it yet. She was rather enjoying the break from email and Facebook. Nothing was pressing enough in her life to care about the Internet right now. Real life provided enough intrigue.

She sat down to read the article. The photo image of Samson Jones caught her eye. No wonder her mother had been besotted with him. He had mocha skin much like that of the current president, tight brown curls, and a lovely profile. The shot was taken from the side. He was laughing. Lillian's heart ached to look at him.

The gist of the story was that he had just disappeared December 1st. There was no trace of him. A search had been done of the grounds about the house, and his parents and others looked and called everyone they could think of. He had taken nothing with him but himself and the clothes he had on. The mystery had never been solved, but the reporter and others speculated that he had just left town for a better life or gotten himself killed in a bad part of Montgomery or another big city and disappeared for good. Lillian sighed, knowing those answers weren't right but not knowing what was. The only place to turn to find out more was her grandmother and the journal. It was best to talk to Grand now before it got too late. Dinner was in an hour, and she didn't want to put it off any longer. She just had to be cautious about how much or what she said.

As she stretched and started walking out of the room, her cell phone rang. It was probably Donovan, and she did want to talk to him. She turned around and picked up the phone.

"Hello." She looked at her watch. She needed to make this quick.

"Hey! How's the family? And Alabama?" The sound of his voice made Lillian grin.

"It's great—well, pretty good, but I can't go into the pretty good part right now. I miss you already, and it's only been a few days." She twirled a lock of hair around her finger, thinking her statement was partially true. She had been too busy to miss him much.

"I know. I miss you, too. At least I'm crazy busy right now with this choir practice and with lessons and classes. I don't have time to think about how lonely I am." He got quiet.

"I've been pretty busy, too, believe it or not, and the crazy thing is—I don't know how long I'm going to stay here." She sighed audibly, feeling torn between Pittsburgh and Magnolian. She had to find out what was going on here and whether there was danger to anyone with the nightmares and other warnings she felt she was receiving from—someone somewhere. A shiver ran through her as she thought about it. Even more than that, she felt that Samson might need her help. Why wait until now to haunt the house? Was it because of the connection she had with her mother—and that they looked alike? Or had he haunted others there? No one had given any indication of that—other than her aunt mentioning her mother's nightmares.

Donovan continued, pulling her out of her reverie. "Well, I have some good news for you. I'm coming down at Thanksgiving just for a few days—if you'll have me, I mean, or if your family will allow it. I figure I can get out of town then before things get too crazy with musical practices. Besides, I need a break." He laughed.

"Donovan! Yes, please come. I can't wait! I'm sure Grand would love you." She spun in a little circle and laughed.

"With that response, how could I refuse? Well, it's what, November 12th today, so I'll be there a couple days before Thanksgiving if I can make it happen." He sounded happy.

"I can't wait! I have to go now. Grand needs me." Telling the little white lie felt okay because, in a way, it might be true. Maybe she did need her.

"All right, Alabama girl. Take care."

"You, too," Lillian said softly and ended the call. Still smiling, it didn't dawn on her until she was in the hallway that the current date was close to the date all those years ago that Samson Jones had disappeared, that her mother had been in love.

Maybe that was why he was appearing to her, singing, and the rest. There was something she needed to know, something that threatened her and those she loved at Magnolian. Troubled, she continued down the hall, not prepared to face Grand, but knowing she must. Hopefully, she could get some answers without being too obvious about what was happening to her.

She tapped on Grand's door, thinking the hallway was too quiet. The house was silent with that waiting kind of listening she had noticed before. Grand's room was silent, too. "Grand?" She tapped more loudly and then opened the door, frightened now, knowing that Grand's nap time was always until around five in the afternoon. She should still be in her room unless she had done something out of the ordinary, which was possible, Lillian reminded herself. She was new to the house. Perhaps Grand didn't always nap like this.

The door opened with a creak, and Lillian gasped. Her Grand was sprawled out on the floor, not moving. Hesitating only a moment, Lillian ran from the room yelling for help. She grabbed her cell phone from her pocket and punched 911, relaying the situation to the dispatcher and hanging up to wait with Grand. She heard steps pounding up the steps, and Leticia burst in.

"What's all the hollering about? What's wrong?" She looked at the floor. "Oh, Miz Stark. She's had one of her spells. Did you upset her?" Leticia glowered at Lillian, putting her hands on her narrow hips.

"No, of course not! I just came to her room to chat, and I couldn't get her to answer and—"

"Never mind," Leticia said, frowning. "She'll be okay. Did you call 911?"

"I did. Was that the right thing to do? I just didn't know if I was alone in the house or how serious she is." Lillian twisted her hands , worried about Grand.

"Yes, better safe than sorry. I think I hear their sirens now. They'll be up in a minute. Better clear out of the way." Leticia walked outside, and Lillian followed her into the far end of the hallway.

The paramedics came through the door and rushed upstairs just moments later. Lillian stood outside the door, praying. She had just lost her father. She couldn't lose Grand, too. Soon, she heard murmuring from the bedroom and recognized Grand's feeble voice.

"I'm fine. Just get me back to my own bed. I don't want to go to the hospital tonight. I won't go!" The high-pitched, querulous sound was unusual for her grandmother. Then again, she had just passed out and probably had had a scare when she awoke to people working on her. Lillian wondered what had happened before Grand had passed out. She knew now would not be a good time to talk with Grand. Instead, she figured she would return to her room now that Grand was in bed and would soon be sleeping or at least resting. She would grab a jacket and head out for a quick walk before dinner.

When she got to her room, she noticed things had been moved. Her purse was sprawled on the bed half open, a tube of lipstick hanging out and her wallet poking out from the unzipped top. The sheets were mussed as well. Had someone been searching her room for something? She immediately thought of her mother's journal and darted to the bookshelf, hoping the would-be thief had not located it. Her fingers hit air when she stuck them in the cranny at the end of the bookshelf. The intruder had taken her mother's journal, but why? And who could have done it?

She threw on a cardigan and headed outside to think. Her best bet was probably to play dumb and not mention that anything was missing. As she reached the front door, she heard voices outside. Joe Tate's bass voice assaulted her ears. He was talking to Percy on the front porch.

"What I need to know is can I count on you, then, Percy, to drum up some primary votes for me among your people?" He stood with his hands on his hips, looking intense.

Lillian was incredulous at the condescension in his tone. Percy appeared not to notice it and replied simply, "Yes sir. I'll do that, sir." She wondered if his tone was an act—put on for men like Joe Tate to keep them off of his back. Knowing Percy, she thought it might be. He was too smart to be bullied around by a guy like Tate.

Joe Tate clapped him soundly on the back and then looked at her.

"How's your grandmother? Heard she took a spill just now?" He looked at her with curious eyes, sweat dripping from his forehead.

"She's resting now. I think she's okay." Lillian brushed past him, needing to get away to think.

"Glad to hear it. Well, I guess I'll get going. I got a lot to do tonight. Bye for now, y'all." He ambled toward his shiny red Ford truck as Lillian headed behind the house. She wondered when he had reached the house. Was it before Grand had fainted and someone had taken the journal?

She rounded the house as she heard Joe Tate's truck start up. She watched the sun begin its final descent into darkness. The fiery orange clouds belied the chill of the evening. Lillian decided to take the path she had walked her first day here, whether she heard Samson's voice or not, for she knew the melancholy song must be his. Perhaps if she could catch a glimpse of him, she could figure out what had happened to him and how that connected with her mother and the inhabitants of Magnolian. She did not relish feeling the oppressive presence of his spirit, but she knew she needed to find out why he was appearing to her.

She found the path easily, remembering the pine needles heaped near its entrance, probably past evidence of raking interrupted. She walked down the path slowly, breathing the smell of cold earth. The sun was setting like a radioactive orange almost directly in front of her. She squinted to avoid looking in to it. About halfway up the path, she saw a person dart across.

"Hey!" She yelled at the figure. He or she looked like a child. Maybe it was someone who worked here at Magnolian or a kid from down the road, exploring the dirt paths. Whoever it was, they were not up ahead now. They had seemingly vanished into thin air, but she knew that wasn't possible.

She wasn't sure if she saw a shadow or not up ahead. Everything got very still and silent as it had before. She stopped on the path, clenching her fists and resolving not to be afraid. Whoever Samson had been in life, he was the same in death. He needed her help, not her fear. As she stood blinking and hoping the shadowy form would solidify further into human shape—or prove to be something else— she felt a hard crack on her head, and everything went pitch black.

She awoke some time later, shivering and disoriented. Her face was caked with dirt on the left side. She could feel the grime in her mouth. Her head was pulsing like a slow-beating, painful heart. She groaned and sat up slowly. It was so dark she couldn't see her hand in front of her face, and there were no stars out tonight. She stumbled to her feet in what felt like slow motion, every step painful. Not only was her head pounding, but her hip hurt as well, probably from where she had fallen. She knew someone had hit her on the head, but why? After what seemed an eternity and thousands of small steps, she made it to the head of the trail, where she could see the twinkling lights of Magnolian. Perhaps in the shuffle of Grand's health scare this afternoon, she had been forgotten. Then she heard a voice calling as she looked at her watch. It was seven o'clock—after dinner. She had been out for an hour or so.

"Miss Lillian! Is that you? Are you okay?" Percy's figure ran across the lawn, the light from the house distorting his shadow, making him appear much taller than he was.

"Yes, it's me," she croaked, her throat dry as she stumbled, trying to walk.

Percy came alongside her and supported her on his arm as she walked slowly and painfully back to the house. They went through the long-dead garden's path in the back of the house to the back door since it was faster.

"What happened, Miss Lillian? Do you remember?" Percy's eyes were big with concern.

"Yes. Someone hit me on the head. But before that, I saw a young man or someone in the woods." She leaned against Percy, feeling lightheaded and woozy.

"Oh, that was Timmy. He's a boy that works for me some nights. He's a little slow, but he don't mean no harm." Percy looked thoughtful.

"Okay, anyway, I was walking down the path, and I stopped to—I stopped to look at a plant, and the next thing I knew, I felt a hard crack on my head. That's it. I must have blacked out for an hour or so after that." Her head felt like it had been broken open and scooped out.

"Well, let's get you on upstairs. Leticia can bring you some dinner in bed on a tray. Most everybody else is upstairs, but Mr. Will is here. He came to check on Grand, and he asked me where you were. Then I got to thinking I hadn't seen you for a while. Just came out to look for you while he went up and looked in on her." They made their through the library to the sitting room where Will stood up like a shot.

"Lily! There you are. I was worried sick about you. What happened? You look like hell." He brushed dirt off of her face and helped her sit on the couch in the dimly lit sitting room.

"I got whacked on the head. Oh, and thanks for the compliment. I guess I've been told worse." Lillian tried to wink, but it came out as a grimace. "Anyway, I'm fine. How's Grand doing?"

"She looks a lot better than you do. That's for sure." Will sat beside her and breathed out heavily. "Now the question is, who hit you on the head and why?" He felt tenderly around on Lillian's head until he got an angry "Ouch!"

"I don't know. I have no idea." She was scared to say more when her biggest suspect was his father. The why behind that, she didn't know. What reason did Joe Tate have to hurt her or keep her off of the path? She felt a light bulb go off in her already aching head. Perhaps that was it. The person who had knocked her out had not wanted her on the path or in the woods for a reason. She knew one thing she could do now was to find that journal. If someone in the house had taken it, it would be here. Perhaps she would have to wait until morning, but she could search each room thoroughly on the off chance that it was hidden here at Magnolian.

"Well, I don't like any of this. I think we should call the police and have them come out here and look around tonight." Will's mouth was set in a stubborn line.

She put her hand on his arm. "No. It's okay, Will. I'm fine. I don't want to bring the police into it." And she didn't, not yet. She wanted the attacker to think he or she was safe. That was her only real chance of finding out who had done it and why.

She took his hand, "Will, I think I'm going to turn in. Has anyone seen Aunt Lorelei, by any chance?" she asked, trying to keep a casual tone. It was hard to even think straight with her head pounding out a drum solo, so she didn't know how casually her voice had come out.

"Yes, Miss Lillian. I sure did. She's gone to the pharmacy to pick up a refill on Miz Stark's medication. She was almost out. She should be back in a half hour or so. Anyway, you take care tonight, and if you need anything, you give me a holler," Percy said as he walked toward the front door. He shut it quietly behind him, and Lillian appreciated that with her head pounding incessantly. She was only hoping she could get rid of Will so easily. He seemed determined to fuss over her. He was asking her if she wanted an ice pack when she turned back in to him.

"Earth to Lily? Are you listening? You look like you're on another planet." He held up two fingers in front of her face. "How many?"

"Two," Lillian groaned with a half smile. "Honestly, I'm just exhausted. I need to get to bed. I'll call you tomorrow and let you know how I'm doing." She smiled at him. "Thanks for everything— for checking on Grand and trying to baby me, too."

"Well, I'm sorry, but you can't go to bed yet. You might have a concussion. I'm at least staying here with you for a while to nurse you and make sure you don't pass out. March it into the living room, and we can watch some television after I get you some pain medication." He walked her to the living room and deposited her on the couch. Then, he walked quickly toward the kitchen and came back with Advil and a glass of water. He sat next to her on the couch and pushed a strand of hair behind her ear.

"I'm fine. Really. I need to do something, and I'll come back and sit with you. Just give me a few minutes." She got up before he could say anything.

Will frowned but didn't protest.

Lillian headed toward the steps. She might not be spry, but if she hurried, she could at least search Aunt Lorelei's room tonight for her mother's journal. Will wouldn't see her from the living room either.

She reached the landing after what seemed like an hour and turned left toward her aunt's room. It was the one across from Grand's. She turned the knob slowly and soundlessly and pushed the door, and her heart tripped faster when she realized it was unlocked. She had never been in this room, and its all-white wicker and girlish pink rosebuds on the white comforter made her shudder. What was a fifty-something-year-old woman doing with a bedroom like this? It was as if she had never moved beyond age twelve. Lillian shoved the night stand drawers open quickly—nothing. She looked under the bed and then tackled the dresser. The journal was secreted in Aunt Lorelei's underwear drawer. Lillian wrinkled her nose in distaste as she peeled a large pair of white cotton underpants off of the journal. She shut the drawer soundly after straightening the underpants.

She wasted no time in scurrying quietly across the room, opening the door, and moving as fast as she could down the hall. She did not want to be caught taking the journal back, even though she had been the one to find it in the first place. After securing the lock and bolt on her door, she sighed in relief and slowly changed out of her clothes, head pounding. She put on her pajamas, figuring Will could deal with it. She hoped she could get rid of him quickly tonight and get back to her mother's journal.

She walked slowly back downstairs, the throbbing in her head easing off a bit. Will patted the couch beside him, and she sat down. He put his arm around her, and she didn't resist snuggling up beside him as they watched something mindless that she couldn't have told the name of the next day. Her head was too foggy. She surrendered to it and just sat there, feeling the strong beat of his heart. They sat like that, more or less, until just after Aunt Lorelei came back. Will looked at Lillian and said, "I think you're okay. I'm going now. Is that all right?" He touched her chin, looking into her eyes.

"Yes, that's fine. I'm going straight to bed anyway." She gave him a wobbly smile. He walked her upstairs to her room, frowning when she turned the key in the lock.

"Why'd you lock it?"

"Oh, I've done that since I was a kid. Just a habit I have." She smiled brightly at him, hoping he believed her. She figured he had seen some good liars in his time, and she wasn't one of them. He didn't seem inclined to argue over it, though.

"All right. Whatever. Take care, Princess, and lock it for tonight.

That's a good idea." He touched his lips to hers, gently. She was so tired she didn't resist.

After she heard him drive away, she settled down in her room, locking the door again and grabbing the journal. She flipped hurriedly through the old pages, taking care, though, not to tear or damage them. She found the next entry: June 20, 1973.

I have finally found a way to talk with him. Every Thursday afternoon, Percy has S. clear cutting and taming the brush in the woods nearer to the house. No one is there but him once he gets going and Percy leaves. Yesterday, I went to him. I walked right up to him and said hello. He smiled and said hi to me. Then, we talked naturally, as if we'd known each other all our lives. I know mama and daddy would be so angry, but he is just like me—human and wonderful. And he wants to be something—to go to college here in town in another year when he has saved up more money. He didn't tell me that, but Lorelei did once. I can't wait to talk with him about it. I told him I'd meet him next week same time and same place.

Lillian breathlessly turned the next page with a soft snick.

June 26, 1973

I met him again today. He brought me a book that he enjoyed: The Tenant of Wildfell Hall by Anne Bronte. I think I'll like it, too, as he said it's an unhappy love story—like most are. We went deep into the woods along a little dirt path to be alone after he was done with the brush cutting. We only had a half hour, but he is fine with me coming again next week. He was angry at first, thinking that I was trying to play some sort of game with him. I think I assured him I'm not.

Lillian's heart was hammering in her chest at the implications of the relationship her mother had had at such a young age and in this place. Suddenly, she heard the door knob turning. She shoved the book under her bedspread, even though she knew the door was locked and no one could get inside. Who was roaming the hall at this hour? Her aunt? The handle jiggled once more, and then heavy footsteps moved down the hall, the sound of Aunt Lorelei's plodding. A door closed down the hall softly. Lillian breathed out and picked the journal up again. The entries were blank for another couple months. The next one was dated August 30, 1973, and was written in what appeared to be a rushed hand:

I am gloriously happy today. S. gave me a ring—a simple, thin, gold band that he saved up to buy at Woolman's in town. I can only wear it on a gold chain close to my heart, but with the ring, he asked me to marry him. I said yes. We will keep our engagement a secret until Christmas when we will tell everyone. If we must leave together, we will. I will do anything to be with him. I know we can make it; we love each other that much.

Lillian felt a tear drop on to the page, knowing that Samson and Gretchen never were together. They hadn't had to run off, and they had never married. She wondered now if her mother had been truly happy or in love with her father. She would like to think that she had been, but she had only his word to vouch for it since she had been only three when her mother had died in a car accident involving a drunk driver. She only knew that her father had been very much in love with her mother. She sighed and read on:

November 1, 1973

These weeks have flown by with school and seeing S. I am happier than I've ever been, and we just know everything is going to work out—that our parents will bless our life together. They have to, or we will leave. Samson has family in Mississippi we could turn to for a while if need be.

Lillian noticed that she was down to the last few pages of the journal, but her eyes would no longer cooperate with her desire to read. She would sleep with the journal tonight. No one would be able to take it from her without waking her up. Perhaps Aunt Lorelei only wanted to read it because she had not known about the romance between Gretchen and Samson when it happened years ago. She tucked the book in the sheets to her left and rolled the sheets up around it. She laughed a little at herself, but then her expression grew somber when she thought about being hit on the head earlier and the headache that still pounded, more gently now after medicine. With a sigh, she turned off the lamp, and the room faded to black.

Chapter 9

They answer and provoke each other's songs—With skirmish and capricious passagings, And murmurs musical and swift jug jug...
—from "The Nightingale" by William Wordsworth

The next week passed by uneventfully apart from the revelations Lillian found in Gretchen's journal. Every night, she locked herself into her bedroom, poring over the pages. She almost felt as if the lives of Samson and Gretchen were more real than her own in these days. Will was busy with court, so he didn't break in to her reading and reverie much. The last three entries of the journal were the most surprising.

November 20, 1973

Thanksgiving is upon us, and we are so busy with decorating the house and picking the recipes we will use this year for the dressing and sweet potato casserole, among other favorites. I am upset and am finding it hard to focus on the season or act as if I'm in tune with what is going on around me. I met S. last week as usual. We were talking afterward on our path near the water tower in the woods when we heard a cracking and snapping of twigs a short distance away. We both went to look to see who might be there, but we saw no one. We only heard someone running away. I fear the onlooker was my sister, but it could have been anyone. Either way, Christmas time can't come fast enough when we will come out in the open with our love for each other...

Lillian almost dropped the journal when she got to the part about the water tower. No wonder the woods had felt inhabited to her. Perhaps Samson was going back to the old place he and Gretchen had spent many happy hours in. And what to make of Gretchen's suspicions of Lorelei? Had she been the one in the woods spying on them, or had it been someone else? After that entry, only two remained before the journal went silent.

November 30, 1973

Thanksgiving is over and thank heavens! I didn't get to see S. for over a week, and every day felt like a life time. The only dark cloud over us is that I'm sure that Joe Tate and my sister know about our relationship. Joe gave me more than one hateful look when he came over for dinner on Thanksgiving evening, and he made more jokes than usual about "the niggers" as he delightfully calls them. Mother and father told him that was enough of his talk, but I know it was intended for me to hear. I'm afraid he is going to do something or tell my parents or Samson's before I get the chance to.

So, Joe Tate had known or likely had known, and perhaps he had found out from Lorelei, or maybe Gretchen was just paranoid by that point. Her secret was a huge one to keep, and she was on the brink of running away with Samson if need be. That would put stress on anyone, and perhaps that was the reason for the paranoid tone in this entry, though Gretchen certainly had reason to feel that way, Lillian reflected, thinking of her own head and her attacker. The last entry in the journal was cryptic and sad, because Lillian knew what much of it referred to.

December 1, 1973

S. has disappeared. Last night, we got to meet near the water tower. It was late, and I had sneaked out of my room. A long bed sheet works quite well—even from a great height! I am not sure if Lorelei heard me or what, but S. and I were talking about the future, just being together, when we heard hoots and hollers in the woods. We both knew they were for us, and we took off running—I in my nightgown and no shoes and he in his trousers with no shirt. I ran along the path, and eventually the loud voices stopped. Someone is making our lives miserable, and now S. is gone. It is as if he has vanished without a trace—into thin air, like a ghost. I fear the worst. Every time I think of him, it is as if I know he is dead. I can't eat a bite, and I stayed home from school today because word spread that he was gone, and I was sick with worry. Mama didn't seem to suspect anything. She thinks I'm just sick with a touch of the flu.

The last entry explained her dream and told about when Samson had gone missing, but Lillian wished there were more entries. She supposed, though, that Gretchen had gone silent, nursing her pain privately until she could forget enough to go on with a normal life. She wondered how much her father had known about her mother's great love before him.

She checked on Grand often and spent afternoons with her on the porch, otherwise keeping to herself and ignoring Aunt Lorelei's sideways, sharp glances. She kept her door locked at all times when she was not there, carrying the little key with her. Will was so busy with court week that he did not bother her much, and she was grateful. Her feelings for him were confusing, and she needed space to think about everything. Donovan would also be arriving on the 23rd. He had called to tell her he had plane tickets and would be renting a car to drive down from Montgomery to Everwood. There were Thanksgiving preparations to make and other distractions as well.

That afternoon, after Donovan called, Lillian went in to talk with Grand. She wanted to broach the topic of her mother and Samson, but she didn't know how. Her grandmother was feeling much better now, and she had never had chance to talk with her about Gretchen's past—other than in passing moments.

She sat by Grand's bedside, before her nap, holding her hand. Grand reclined, smiling and alert, wearing her prettiest yellow nightgown.

"Grand, can you tell me about Mother when she was a teenager? What was she like? Did she have a boyfriend? I've always wanted to know about her, and father told me about her life when he met her, but there's so much he might not have known. I guess that's part of the reason I'm here—to find her and me." Lillian stopped abruptly, not wanting to say too much or to indicate what she had read in the journal.

Grand got a faraway look about her. "Well, your mother was always spirited. She lived, it seemed, to go against the grain." Grand's violet eyes clouded with memories of the past, and she frowned. "There were so many times she almost got herself into trouble she couldn't get out of."

"Oh, really? What did she do?" Lillian tried to hide her rising excitement. She smoothed the covers over Grand's legs and sat back in her chair, putting a neutral expression on her face, she hoped.

"Oh, she was just good at giving people a piece of her mind. She and Joe Tate never got along, you know? That's just one person or situation I can think of." Grand's laughter tinkled like a music box. "She always hated his racist jokes and remarks, and she would often tell him so. I don't think he liked that very much. I don't think he liked her at all, in fact." Grand's face darkened. Then, she smiled. "But that's all in the past, dear. Joe is part of the family, and he has such ties to Magnolian. I don't know if your mother ever understood that really."

Lillian thought, I don't know if she wanted to understand it. Joe Tate was hateful and unsettling, and it seemed her mother had been wise in disliking him.

"Did my mother have a lot of boyfriends, Grand?" She smiled, but she felt like she would scream if she couldn't get more out of Grand than this.

Grand frowned, her eyes moving in thought. "You know, she didn't have a real boyfriend until she was in college—at least that she told me about—but I always thought there was someone, well, someone she cared about when she was in high school—at least for part of it. She went through a withdrawn phase, but she always had this secret happiness about her. And I know she sneaked out of the house one evening because Lorelei told on her. I didn't punish her or even say anything about it. I knew your mother was a good girl at her core and that if she had done that, there was a reason." Grand smiled at her and patted her hand. "Kind of like you are, Lillian."

Lillian felt a lump in her throat at the love and trust Grand had displayed and still did.

"Who do you think she was in love with? You didn't have any ideas?" She held her breath.

"I don't know. I honestly don't, and I guess I never will. I think it was someone she thought we wouldn't have approved of, but I loved her. If that someone made her happy and she could make a life with him, I would never have disapproved." A tear rolled down Grand's cheek. "Sometimes, I wish she had opened up to me more." Her voice trailed off, and Lillian could see that she was exhausted by the conversation.

Lillian hugged her grandmother, thinking that her viewpoint was certainly unexpected and progressive for the times. It was too bad that her own mother hadn't realized how much she was loved. "Grand, I think she knows you wish that. Somehow, I just think she does." Tears spilled out of Lillian's eyes, and she brushed them away, not wanting the other woman to see them. So, her grandmother really didn't know anything about Samson Jones and Gretchen, not unless she was a very skilled liar, and Lillian didn't think so.

She noticed that Grand's eyes were getting heavy, so she kissed her on the cheek.

"I'll see you at dinner, Grand—if you come downstairs. I love you."

"I love you, too, Lillian. I'm so glad you came to see me." She snored lightly a moment later.

Lillian padded out of the room and down the hall, feeling at a loss. She had a sense of urgency—that the ghostly visitations and the recurring dream, as well as the thump on the head, indicated that she was getting close to answers about Samson's disappearance. She needed another head, though, to help her figure out where to go from here—how to find out the rest of the story and figure out who wanted to keep her from doing so. She unlocked the door to her room and sat on her bed, deep in thought. She didn't want to wait three more days for Donovan to arrive on the 23rd. She needed someone to talk to now that she trusted enough to confide some of the story in. Will's face popped into her head. After their initial rough patch, he had been such a good friend to her, and he hadn't pushed for more than she had been willing to give. Taking a deep breath, she picked up her cell phone.

She had his number programmed in. Amber answered, smacking gum.

"I'll tell him you called," she drawled in a sugar sweet tone.

Lillian hung up with a smile. That returned call would probably be a while in coming. Thinking that she might as well do something constructive with her day, Lillian decided to borrow Grand's BMW and go job hunting. She needed to think of her own future, and it was getting too easy to get wrapped up in a mystery that was over forty years old while her own life passed her by. As she felt more sure about who she was and where she was going, she realized that she didn't want her future to be accidental, but intentional. Her mother's death, her father's death, and other things were beyond her control, but she would not be a victim of chance or fate. Squaring her shoulders, she went into her bathroom, touched up her makeup, and headed downstairs. She grabbed the keys to the BMW from the drawer where they were kept. Grand had told her to take the car any time, but she only had taken it to run errands twice so far, and she was, apparently, the only one who drove the car—and walked out the front door. The day was considerably colder, and she was glad she had worn her red scarf. She pulled it tightly around her neck.

As she exited the garage, she caught a glimpse of Timmy, a strange-looking boy with a thick forehead and large eyes, really a slender man. Lillian wondered if he was who she had seen earlier in the woods. She had never talked to him because he skulked around mostly. He gave her the creeps, though she felt bad for thinking that way. He was just slow. It was good that he was gainfully employed at Magnolian, and Percy seemed to like him.

Waving at Percy, who was exiting the shed as she got rolled away, she quickly turned the heater up high. She drove through the pillars of Magnolian, enjoying the sight of sunlight glinting through the nearly bare pine trees. She loved the blue skies here and knew that back in Pittsburgh, it was gray most of the time now. Donovan had even grumbled about it yesterday. She smiled, thinking of him, and turned left onto the highway headed into town.

She had picked up some speed and touched the brake to slow down for the entrance into town. Nothing happened. She mashed the brake again, starting to panic. She was coming up behind a line of cars at the red light that signaled the start of Everwood. She punched the brake one more time. Realizing that the brakes were out, she coasted more quickly than she would have liked to the side of the road into a bunch of bushes. The impact was harder than she expected, and she felt the air bag deploy. She sat in stunned silence for a minute. How could the brakes have gone out on the car? She knew that Percy maintained Grand's vehicle well and checked everything scrupulously. She remembered spending an afternoon with him working on the cars. She also knew that he would not entrust something like that to Timmy. He had told her Timmy only did the simplest of tasks as needed outside.

She was brought out of her reverie and shock by a tapping on the car window. It was Joe Tate. Her first thought was how did he happen to get here first? She just sat there, looking at him. The whole episode seemed surreal, but the car in the brush was real enough.

He opened the car door.

"Are you hurt? Don't need to move if you're hurting anywhere." He looked her over and shook his head, his thick cheeks moving in the breeze.

"I don't think so. I am just a little stiff and sore. Could you just help me out? I guess I need to call Percy or a tow truck or something." Lillian unfolded from the car on legs as shaky as a baby's. Joe Tate took her hand in his big paw and helped her lean against the car. The air outside felt good and helped clear her head a bit.

"Don't worry about a thing. Already done it as soon as I saw the car over here."

"How did you know it was me?" Lillian's voice came out high pitched, like a crazy woman's. Settle down, she told herself. Don't get paranoid over something that could have happened naturally. After all, it was a small town, and people drove past this point multiple times a day.

"Oh, I didn't. I just knew it was Beverly's car. I thought she might be in it." He looked at her, hands on his hips, lips pursed.

She swallowed hard, not willing to let it go. "But she—she never drives anymore."

"Oh? I didn't know that. At any rate, it's good I came by. What happened anyway? Talking on your cell phone and ran off the road?" He sneered.

"No, I wasn't. The brakes failed. I tried them several times, and they just wouldn't work when I tried to stop." She looked at him, her cheeks hot and her brow furrowed in anger.

"What? Oh, well, things happen. Maybe old Percy hasn't checked the car out in a while." He rolled his eyes as if he were making a certain statement about men like Percy—black men.

"I don't think so. He maintains everything well, and Grand has trusted him for so many years." Lillian's voice was clipped. "Well, anyway, I do appreciate you calling everyone and for staying with me until someone gets here." She walked a step away from the car.

"Yeah, I was glad to do it. I called Will, too. He just got out of court and should be here any minute to pick you up and take you back to Magnolian or wherever you need to go. I'll wait here with you 'til he shows up." He spread his legs as he leaned harder against the car.

They waited in silence, Lillian shaking a little from cold and shock. Did car brakes just go out, even with good maintenance? She didn't think so. And if not, someone had just tried to kill her or at least hurt her bad enough to put her out of commission. After what seemed like hours, Will pulled up on the side of the road and jumped out of the car, sprinting toward her. He looked cool and collected, even after a full day in court, in a black suit and red tie.

"Lily! Are you okay? What happened?" His eyes looked wild.

"The brakes failed. I don't know why, but they didn't work when I tried to stop at the intersection." She sighed, just wanting to sit down somewhere. Will frowned at her.

"Let me take a look. I know something about cars. I fix my own and have built one or two."

He popped the hood of the car and went around to look under it. As he did, Joe Tate waved and walked back to his truck.

"Take care, Lillian," he called. "You seem to be accident prone these days, girl."

She lifted a hand in a curt wave, not saying anything.

"Yep, the brake line's been cut clean through," Will called. He whistled. "Somebody really doesn't like you, Lily." He walked back around to her and stood beside her, looking at her, brows furrowed. She didn't say anything.

Just then, the towing service pulled up, and Will ordered them to take the car to a local garage to check the brakes out and confirm his suspicions. After they pulled away with the BMW in tow, he put his arm around Lillian and walked her to his car. She got in gratefully and rested her head against the seat, closing her eyes. "Thank you so much. I really needed to sit down."

Will got into the car in silence.

"Where to?" Make it a good drive because I want to know what the hell is going on and who it is who's trying to kill you or at least hurt you real bad." Will lapsed into a full Southern drawl.

"Let's go out near the water tower again. I can't believe I'm saying it, and I don't like the feel of the place, but there's a reason. Do you have a blanket or something in the back?"

"You know it." He grinned devilishly.

"I just need it to wrap up in. I'm cold," Lillian said, rolling her eyes.

"Are you sure you don't need to get checked out at the hospital? If so, let's stop there first."

"No, I'm fine—just shaken up." They pulled back on to the highway.

Will called Magnolian and told Leticia that he had picked up Lillian and that they would be out for a while. He reassured her that Lillian was fine, and Lillian felt loved, hearing the fussing on the other end of the line. So Leticia really wasn't as cold as she seemed. How interesting and surprising, but then, how could you ever really know anyone?

They drove a couple miles back down the highway. The sky was darkening with the last rays of the day. The flaming sun that had been out earlier was nowhere to be found. Lillian shivered as they pulled into the small dirt road that led to the water tower. When they got there, Will parked and dug a thick, ragged quilt out of the trunk. They made their way to the water tower and sat down, thinking it would be too cold to sit in the woods along the dirt path. The shading of the trees would drop the temperature even lower.

Will sat down next to her on the grass as she wrapped up in the quilt. The wind picked up as they got settled, swirling a few golden leaves in its wake and rustling the bushes like a lover's sad sigh.

"Okay, now start at the beginning. Tell me everything because I want to hear it. What's going on? Or do you know?" Will looked at her, reflections of dark trees swaying in his pale eyes.

"I think I do—know what's going on, I mean. It's a long story, so let me start with the ghost in my room, the same one in the woods, and the journal I found." She sighed, feeling him tense up beside her, and who wouldn't? Even mentioning the word *ghost* was setting herself up for it, but she had to make him understand the nature of what had been happening—both human and supernatural.

"Ghost?" He raised his voice in disbelief. "Lily, no ghost cut the brake line." Seeing her grim face above the frayed, red quilt, he put his hands on his head and leaned them on his knees. "Don't look at me like that. Okay, I'll listen—ghosts and all. Just tell me what's been going on. I'm worried about you," he finished, tearing a blade of grass out of the ground and obliterating it into tiny pieces. The water tower stood above them, a silent white witness.

Lillian recounted the story, telling him about the shadowy shape in her room, the singing in the woods, her mother's journal, the disappearance of Samson Jones, and about being hit on the head near the spot she had heard the ghost singing days before. She told it all slowly because she couldn't think fast after the wreck and because she didn't want to leave anything out. She wanted to convince him, no needed to. She needed an ally here in Everwood, and he was the only one she thought she could trust, or at least the only one who was willing and able to help her.

"And you remember here when you made a pass at me and I got upset? You remember what I said I felt here?" She asked, looking at him with big eyes.

"Yes, of course I do, though I'd like to forget it. I know, though, women never forget." Will rolled his eyes, waiting for her to finish.

"Stop it. I'm serious, Will. I felt Samson's spirit here that day, too—his presence. Everything got still, and I felt such a sadness. I can't describe it, but I could tell you didn't feel it. I just had to get out of here, like I told you before." She closed her eyes against the memories.

"If it's so awful, then why are we here now?" He looked at her with no humor lurking in his face.

"I needed to face this place again, and it's private. Besides, Samson is friendly. I just know he is after reading about all of it. He's in need, but he's not malicious, just sad. I think the person who killed him is still dangerous, and he's trying to save me, or maybe even Magnolian. As crazy as all of that sounds, I'm sure of it, Will." A single tear slipped down Lillian's cheek. She brushed it away, knowing she was overwrought from the car accident just a short while ago.

"Okay, hold on, hold on, hold on." Will put his hands up like a referee calling on a bad play. You said that someone killed him. You don't know that. All you have is a newspaper article, Fanny's word, and a journal by a lovesick girl that prove he went missing. Maybe he just left—took off because the pressure of being with your mother was too much, or maybe he was just sick of Everwood. Lord knows I can see how a black man might hate this place." Will leaned his chin on his now-dirty knees and pants and wrapped his arms around them, looking at her. She could tell he was puzzling it all over.

"Sure, I get what you're saying, but that doesn't explain why someone has been trying to hurt me." She glared at him as a spider landed on his shoulder. She brushed it off, her hand lingering on his arm for a moment.

"I know, so there must be something to what you are saying. That's what bothers me. My main concern is keeping you safe." Will looked at her, and lifting her hand, kissed it.

"Thanks. I want to stay safe, but I need to know what happened to Samson—for me and for Grand and everyone at Magnolian." Lillian lifted her chin with a show of determination. "And you know it's going to take more than a conk on the head and a shoddy brake cut to make me leave here or quit trying to figure it out. This was my mother's home, and no one is going to run me out like that." Her voice had grown shrill, and her eyes snapped with violet flames.

Will sighed. Lillian noticed that the woods had gone unnaturally still. The flesh on her back crept. She spoke softly, "Samson, I know you're here, and I'm going to help you. I promise." The woods around her seemed to sigh plaintively. Will just looked at her like she was nuts. She stood up, brushing leaves off of her jeans and shaking the quilt out. The air felt thick and full of sadness. It was almost more than she could stand after the day she had had.

"I need to get back to the house. Everyone will be wondering about me, especially the person who cut my brakes—if that person is at Magnolian." She glanced sideways at Will, wondering if he caught her drift. He didn't seem to, and she had carefully left out the parts about his father in her story. She planned to talk with him tomorrow when Will was out of the office or in a meeting with just the two of them. She wanted to surprise Joe and press him on the question of what he had known about Gretchen and Samson, if anything, as her mother had suspected in her journal.

"Thanks for trusting me enough to tell me what's going on," Will said, stowing the quilt in the trunk and getting in the car as she did, moving more slowly. Her aches and pains from the accident were starting to make themselves known by shouting. The short ride to Magnolian was a quiet one with each of them lost in their thoughts. When they drove down the driveway, warm lights twinkled in the house, belying the strange events that had taken place in recent days. Lillian paused before getting out, reveling in the safety of Will's car.

"All right, here's your stop. I'll call you tomorrow. Watch out. Call me if you need anything. I mean it, Lily." Will squeezed Lillian's hand as she moved to open the door.

"Thanks for everything, Will." Lillian smiled as she shut the car door. She stood a moment and stretched her back out before she walked into the house.

A chorus reached her ears: questions asked in tandem from Grand, Aunt Lorelei, and even Leticia as she placed a huge pot of steaming chili on the sideboard.

Lillian raised her hand to silence them all. "Yes, I'm okay. I appreciate your concern for me. I really do." She teared up, and her voice grew thick. "Right now, I just want to have a bowl of chili and go upstairs to rest. I could use some Advil, too, if you have it around. I seem to be needing it a lot lately," she said. Leticia bustled out to find the medicine as Lillian crumpled into a chair where a bowl of hot chili topped with cheese and onions waited for her. A slice of fresh whole-wheat bread sat near the bowl. Despite her bruises and tender spots, Lillian was hungry, and she dug right in.

"Lillian, I don't know how to tell you this, but—" Grand's voice sounded strained. "The mechanics that took a look at my car said it had been tampered with. The brake line was most certainly cut. They called a little while ago." Grand looked tired, her eyes shadowed and her mouth turned down.

"Oh. I figured that, Grand." Lillian didn't have anything else to say, and she didn't want the perpetrator, if he or she were at the table or within hearing distance, to hear her go into flights of hysteria.

Eyes swiveled her way. "That's all you have to say! You might have been killed!" Aunt Lorelei turned a muddy, disapproving eye toward Lillian as she slurped chili.

"I know, but I wasn't, and it's over now. Maybe the brake line got cut by accident somehow. I'm sure it has happened." The silence around the table was full of disbelief.

Lillian finished half of the bowl and drank another sip of sweet tea. "I'm tired. I'm going to excuse myself now. Thanks for coming down to dinner to check on me, Grand and everyone. I'm fine." She looked them all one last time. Leticia and even Percy were hanging around the dining room to see how she had fared. Lillian went over and hugged her grandmother hard.

"We love you dear. I'm so glad you're all right." Grand's eyes twinkled, tears threatening to fall. "Oh, here's Leticia with that medicine." Leticia, her features softened in worry, handed two blue pills to Lillian, who swallowed them quickly.

"Good night, everyone," she mumbled, feeling completely drained. She dragged herself slowly up the stairs, glancing at her mother's shining face as she walked by. She was more and more convinced that the image was of the sixteen-year-old Gretchen—the one who was hopeful for a future with a young man who was out of her social sphere. The heartache of their story was too much for her to bear, and she turned away from the image as she stepped on to the landing. She was happy to open the door to her room, make preparations for bed, and climb in under warm covers. The little calico cat peeped her head out from under the bed where she must have been hiding for quite a while and jumped up, purring to be petted. Lillian held the cat to her, relishing the comfort. She turned the lamp off, knowing she would soon be lost in sleep.

Chapter 10

*And one low piping sound more sweet than all—Stirring the air with
such an harmony, That should you close your eyes, you might almost
Forget it was not day!*
—from "The Nightingale" by William Wordsworth

The 21st of November dawned bleak and colder than previous
weeks. The bedroom was chilly, and Lillian snuggled against the
covers, looking at the alarm clock by the bed: 8:03 a.m. No real
reason to get out of bed immediately. Then she remembered her plan
to see Joe Tate sometime today and sighed. She pulled herself out of
bed, took a quick shower, and dressed in warm corduroy pants and a
black V-neck sweater. She threw her bright pink scarf on for safe
measure and to perk up her exhausted looking face. She also brought
along her long, gray coat. Checking her lipstick in the bathroom
mirror, she picked up her cell phone and dialed the office number
Will had given her some days ago. When Amber answered with a
"Ye-e-es, Tate and Tate. How may I help you-u-u?" multiple syllables
long on every vowel, she asked for Joe Tate, hoping Amber would not
recognize her voice. She didn't seem to, and she connected her with
Joe after a bit of Muzak.

"Joe Tate here." His voice boomed so that Lillian had to turn the
volume on her phone down to avoid hearing loss.

"Joe, it's Lillian Mullins. How are you?" She didn't really care
how he was, but it seemed polite to ask, and she knew an older
Southern gentleman would expect her to. She needed to talk him into
seeing her today.

"Oh, well, now, I'm fine, Miss Lillian, but that's not the real question," he drawled. "I need to know how you're feeling today after your scary day yesterday?" He sounded almost gleeful thinking about it. Of course, that could have just been the cell phone reception, Lillian thought with a tiny smile.

"I'm fine, Joe. Just fine. Nothing a good night sleep didn't cure. Listen, I was wondering if you had time for me to come in and talk with you—privately. If not, could we meet for lunch or coffee somewhere?" Her tone was brisk, but she felt like she needed to be professional to convince this man she wasn't playing around.

"Sure, Honey. I got all the time in the word for you, Sugarpie."

Lillian flinched. "That's great. Thanks so much." She tried to gush, but she just couldn't pull it off like the Southern women who lived here seemed to be able to. Apparently, her gene pool didn't have enough of that gushing marker in it. "What time is best for you, then, Joe?"

"Oh, why don't you come around the office at, say, 12. Will won't be here, so the meeting will be nice and private." The tone of voice Tate used made Lillian's stomach tilt.

"All right. Thank you again for your time today. I'll see you then." She clicked the end button and threw the phone down on her messy, unmade bed, staring into space. She decided she would pass some time on her laptop. She was still feeling out of sorts and didn't feel like a big jaunt this morning. Dealing with Joe Tate would be enough, she had a feeling.

She logged on to Facebook and caught up with the few friends she had in California, Pittsburgh, and just on line in general via other friends or past experiences. She smiled when she noticed a few new friend requests from Everwood folks—Willoughby Eustace Tate being one of them and Fanny Marshall, the historical society employee, another. Eustace? She laughed aloud, thinking it was delicious to know his middle name. She wondered if he loved or hated it. It certainly sounded Southern if nothing else. She'd have to ask next time she saw him—or not. Maybe she would just mention how much she loved the name and wanted all her baby sons named Eustace. She blushed at her own crazy line of thinking. What was wrong with her these days? The guy was still a jerk—a hurting one maybe and a friend at times, but probably still not a nice guy. She was not yet convinced of his goodness. Will's profile picture cracked her up. He was wearing googly-eyed glasses. So, he did have a sense of humor under all that intensity, she thought with a grin. It was hard to stay mad at him over anything.

She spent some time looking through his Facebook photos. One popped up with an hourglass-shaped, tanned, yellow-bikinied Monica at his side. They were both toasting to the camera with expensive imports in hand. The date on the photo was last summer. He certainly looked happy to be with her, Lillian sniffed. She still didn't believe the "just a friend" thing he had said. Other women showed up in his dozens of photos, looking happy and attractive at his side. In fact, women made up the bulk of his photos. She sighed and started to close his page. She didn't want to think about how many other women he had been with and how experienced he was versus her own inexperience. These were just more reasons not to get worked up over a guy. She thought better of it and went to his last page of pictures.

The last three albums were of him and Tansy. Lillian's heart went to her throat. Tansy was gorgeous—a heart-shaped face with fiery red hair and long legs. Shots of them at Niagara Falls, camping in Fort Payne, eating dinner with friends, and other gatherings made her sad. How could she ever live up to a dead woman's memory? Did she even want to try? Donovan would be here in two days—if he was coming still. She closed his page out for good, vowing not to look at his photos again. Facebook was a blessing and a curse, she thought .

After spending too long chatting with an old high school friend who wanted to reconnect, she opened her email. She had applied for a few internships with publishing/writing companies in the Pittsburgh area for her senior year of college before dropping out to care for her father. She wondered if any of them would have gotten back with her yet—if at all.

She was surprised to find an email from a small publishing house, inviting her to begin a position in January on their editing staff—just a couple months away. The promise was for six months with the potential to turn into a full-time position. Lillian sighed. It was good news, but she didn't know if she would be back home by then or if Pittsburgh even was home anymore. She dashed a quick email to them explaining her circumstances and wrote that she definitely was interested in the position, but perhaps not starting on January 2nd. Her heart heavy, she logged off her computer and closed it down.

As she was straightening up the bedroom a bit, collecting clothes that had flown everywhere, seemingly on their own, her phone rang.

"Hey. What's up? I can't believe I'll be there—with you—in two days." Donovan's voice was on the other end, and she could hear him smiling.

"Me neither. I'm psyched. You're going to think you've landed in another world—an alien planet." Lillian laughed as she threw clothes into the hamper by her dresser and grabbed a rag from the dust rags in the closet. She dusted the dresser and bookshelf as they talked.

"Well, I was just checking on you. Everything ok? No more bumps on the head?"

Lillian hesitated, not wanting to say too much and get him alarmed over the phone. He would be here in two days anyway.

"Things are good. We'll talk more when you get here. I'm really looking forward to it. Grand is, too. I gotta go. I have a meeting with a lawyer in town today." She sprayed some polish on the rag and ran it over the bookshelf until it gleamed.

"Uh oh. Sounds like you're already in trouble, and you just got there. All right, have a great day, Lillian. I'll talk to you when I land, most likely. I have a lot of packing to do before then." He laughed .

"See you then. Take care." She hung up the phone, her heart lightened a bit despite the other things going on.

She checked her watch. She just had enough time to grab some brunch before her meeting with Joe. Brushing her hair one last time, she threw the brush on the counter, locked her room, checking the knob twice, and headed down stairs. Luckily, she was the only one wanting to eat. It was between normal meal times, though, so that explained it. Leticia was nowhere to be found in the dining room or sitting room, so Lillian headed toward the kitchen to find sandwich makings. As she reached the closed door to the kitchen, she heard whispering voices.

"What do you think it happened for? It has something to do with my boy—with Samson."

Lillian gasped and put her hand over her mouth as she heard Percy talking.

"I don't know. All I know is it's a bad business, and I'm worried. I don't want nothing like that to happen again around here. Miz Stark couldn't take it. None of us could." Leticia's voice was a shrill whisper.

Lillian decided to walk in and pretend all was well. "Good, well, morning, I guess." She grinned at them both in turn as if she hadn't heard anything.

Looking flustered, Percy grabbed his rake from beside the door and headed out the other way toward the front of the house waving and saying, "Good morning to you, too. I'll see you later, Miss Lillian." He walked out of the kitchen.

"Wait, Percy. Is there a car I take out to town today?" He stopped and looked at her with a worried line between his eyes.

"Sure. You can take my truck. I'll leave the keys on the kitchen table. Nobody's gonna mess with my vehicle." He looked grim as he walked out of the room.

Leticia stood silent, arms crossed, looking at Lillian. "Well, what do you want? I know you heard us talking." Her belligerent tone covered up the fear that Lillian sensed.

"Oh, I missed breakfast. I just came in to get a sandwich. I'll get it, Leticia." She started toward the refrigerator.

"No, you go sit down at the table. You still look funny from yesterday. I'll fix it and bring it out to ya. What kind do you want?" Leticia flapped her arms in a shooing motion toward Lillian.

"Just tuna with mayo will be fine—and some water. Thanks, Leticia." Lillian gave her a long look and then walked out of the kitchen and back into the dining room. Leticia brought her food some minutes later. She plopped the plate and glass down and stood there for a minute.

"Miss Lillian," she said softly, like a statement.

"Hmm?" Lillian answered, with a bite of tuna in her mouth.

"Don't take what I'm saying wrongly. I mean it—for your sake, Miss. I think you should leave here—leave here and never look back. It ain't safe for you here." Leticia spoke with a tremble in her voice.

"You're probably right, but I'm not leaving, not until I find out what's going on around here and what happened to Samson Jones." Lillian spoke matter-of-factly and turned to look at Leticia as she bit into the sandwich again.

Leticia's eyes got big. "You know about Samson?"

"I do—because I was trying to figure out who was singing in the woods and in my room at night and making ghostly appearances in the same places." Lillian raised her eyebrows, looking straight at Leticia.

"Oh my God! Lord save us," Leticia muttered, rolling her eyes. "What are you talking about? I ain't ever heard that," Leticia stammered, but her eyes shifted away from Lillian's.

"Yes, you have. I know my mother complained of the same thing—at least a couple years after Samson disappeared—when she wasn't scared to talk anymore. Well, at least not to everyone. I know she talked to you. She felt she could trust you, didn't she? How many times did she see or hear his ghost?" Lillian locked her eyes on Leticia's, not letting her look away.

"How do you know that? Who told you that? Nobody could

have—Percy wouldn't have. He don't even know what happened between the two of them." Leticia's chin quivered with emotion.

"No one told me. I just guessed it. You've been so standoffish with me ever since I got here—trying to avoid me. I just realized why when I heard you talking with Percy. She told you. You must have been close to her."

"I was. Oh, Miss Lillian. I can't even explain to you how she was. Your mama—she was just something else. Gretchen was a wonderful girl. Nothing like her sister. I was always close with her. I used to fix her hair in the afternoons when she could get out of doing her chores. She was a sneak." Leticia's eyes were alight with memories of a colorful past.

"Anyway, she got older and quieter. She changed like. I just didn't know why, but after she couldn't keep her secret no more, she came to me and told me about how she had been in love with Samson and thought someone had found out and done something to him. Wasn't nothing I could do though but console her. It was a year after it happened before she told me." Leticia's eyes were brimming with tears. Lillian was moved to see the emotion that talking about her mother's struggles brought out in the woman. "As far as I know, he only appeared to her three times, and she couldn't make nothing out of his appearances, but she was also distracted then by happy times, and maybe he just couldn't come to her when she was like that. I don't know." Leticia's gaze was looking far at something—someone—Lillian couldn't see. She sensed, though, that Leticia had told her all she knew.

"Thanks for being honest with me, Leticia. I'm going to find out who hurt Samson and my mother. I won't leave until I do. I know you're worried about me, but I'll be okay. Trust me." Lillian's gaze on Leticia didn't waver.

"All right, Miss Lillian. I'll look out for you the best I can, but you be careful. Someone did something bad once and they'll do it again if it means protecting their own hide!" Leticia left the dining room with hunched shoulders.

Lillian finished her tuna sandwich, took a swig of water, and grabbed Percy's keys, desperate to escape the heavy atmosphere of Magnolian that morning—even if it did mean driving to do it.

The little Ranger pickup truck was fun to drive. She took it slowly down the driveway and kept to a speed of forty-five on the highway, letting several cars pass her. Her heart skittered in her chest, and her palms dripped sweat at the thought of someone messing with another car, but anything was possible. After a drive that took longer than it needed to but on which she got to see the lovely old houses and tidy streets of Everwood, she made it to Tate & Tate. Will's car was noticeably absent from the parking lot, which was a good sign.

Amber ushered her in to Joe Tate's office, and Lillian noticed that her skirt had shortened up even more than its tiny length on her last visit, and the bleached hair was now dark black. I guess it's the changing season, Lillian thought, smirking behind her back. She had to admit, though, that almost anything was better than the stereotypical Southern look she was coming to recognize of a dark, dark tan and bleached blond hair. Amber was obviously a natural brunette.

Joe jumped up from behind his desk, his ample belly jiggling, as she walked into his office. Sporting a red long-sleeved dress shirt, he looked like a strange version of Santa Claus or a country and western singer. Lillian couldn't decide. The shirt put her more at ease for some reason.

"It's always a pleasure to see you, young lady, but what did you need to talk with me about?" He placed a pencil behind his ear as he sat back down after shaking her hand with a sweaty palm.

"I just need to know what you know or remember about Samson Jones." She said it evenly and slowly, looking him straight in the eye.

Joe raised his eyebrows. "Samson Jones, you say? Lessee, that's old Percy's son, ain't it? Well, not much as far as I can remember. He was always a good boy, but he went missing, oh, some thirty-odd years ago. Nobody's heard from him since." He eyed her grimly. "Girl, why in the world do you want to know about him? That's a skeleton best left untouched." She looked at him grimly. "What?" He asked defensively. He had obviously been speaking figuratively of Samson. He shifted in his seat, and Lillian couldn't tell if it was from nerves or restlessness.

"I think my mother had a connection with him, and I think he was hurt or killed for it." She stared at him, unflinching.

"Good Lord, girl. So what if she did have a, as you put it, connection, with him?" He leered, and the word sounded filthy on his tongue. "Ain't none of my business or no one else's if she took up with a, er, a black man. She was a fool if she did, but nobody would kill over that. Don't look good for the family name, though, does it? Mixing races and the like." He grimaced like a righteous minister on a sermon about burning in hell.

Lillian pushed her angry words down, amazed that this man— running for governor no less—could think such hateful things in the twenty-first century. And that after having a black president. "It's important to me to know the whole story. Anything you think you might know or anything you suspect would be helpful to me."

"Well, I sure wish I did know something to help you. You think this is connected to your accidents?" He looked surprised and thoughtful. "If someone hurt him, that person should get justice. That's right by the law." He nodded his head in that know-it-all way once more.

"Yeah, I agree." She let a silence develop and then gave up. Nothing more was forthcoming from him. "I appreciate your time, Joe."

"Sure thing, hon. You stay out of trouble now, you hear? You thinking you might head on back up North? I know Will would hate to see you go, but it seems dangerous for you here lately." His eyes glinted behind his glasses.

"You know, it's curious. You're the second person today who has told me I should leave here, and this is the second time I'll say firmly that no, I'll be staying until I figure out why someone knocked me on the head and tampered with the brakes to the car." Lillian could feel the heat in her face and knew she wanted to leave the office. She stood up and turned toward the door. "Goodbye, Joe. Thanks for everything."

"Bye," he said with a shrug. "Take care."

She walked out of the office smiling as Amber's gum popped, "By-e-e-e."

The cold was still brutal, and the sky was the gray of old putty— uninspiring and nasty. The sun was nothing more than an off-white blot against the leaden clouds. Lillian hurried out to Percy's truck and got in. Just as she was leaving, Will pulled up. She started the car, but he waved at her to stop. She did, sighing. She wasn't sure she wanted to deal with Will this evening. She had such mixed feelings about him. He had been so good to her, but he confused her, too. To add to the confusion, Donovan would be here in a couple days. She smiled to herself. Who would have thought she would have two handsome men vying for her attention? Not her, never in her wildest dreams.

"Lily!" She had rolled the window down, and he stuck his face near hers, smiling. He looked immaculate as always in a white long-sleeved dress shirt and black slacks. His pink tie was a nice touch, and he had the confidence to pull it off where other men would refuse to even try.

"Hey, what's up?" she asked, keeping her voice even.

"I'm mad I missed you. I didn't know you were coming by, or I would have eaten lunch here. I got an invite I couldn't refuse from a girl down the street." He winked and then grew serious.

"How are you? Feeling okay?" He touched her hair, and she could feel the warmth of his hand on her head.

"I'm fine. I didn't want to annoy you today. I've been enough bother lately. I just needed to talk with your father about a legal question I had concerning dad's house." She told the lie without blinking. Her father had always told her she was a terrible liar.

"Since you're here," he traced her cheek to her chin with his finger, and heat seared through her, "why not have dinner with me tonight night? Say my place at seven? I promise I can cook."

"That sounds lovely. I'll be there. Anything you want me to bring?" She forced herself to look unimpressed, but her heart was hammering away.

"Just your lovely self. That's it." He grinned and waved. "It's back to work for me. See you at seven sharp." She watched him walk to the door, admiring his assets in his slacks. She had a feeling he knew she was watching, too.

Sighing, Lillian started the truck up and drove back to Magnolian. The drive went by quickly as pine trees and flat road rushed by her unseeing eyes. She was deep in thought about her conversation with Joe Tate. Had he known more than he was telling? She couldn't tell. Maybe he was a good liar, too. He was certainly a racist, but that might be his only crime. It would be a common one not only here, but anywhere in the United States.

By the time she pulled into the driveway at her grandmother's house, the wind had kicked up and was moaning through the sparsely covered pine trees. A dozen leaves rolled in front of her, scraping the pavement like bones clinking on a chalkboard. She hurried into the front door. Her aunt accosted her three steps into the foyer.

"Are you staying for dinner tonight? Leticia wants to know. She's frying up catfish." Her aunt peered at her with her gimlet eyes. Without a stitch of makeup on, she was even more frightening than usual. Lillian tried to muster up some pity, but it was impossible when she thought about this woman stealing into her room and taking her own mother's journal.

"No, I won't be here. I'm going out, but thanks for asking." She squared her shoulders and strode past the woman. She sensed her aunt's beady eyes on her back as she took the stairs quickly. She planned to spend no more time than she had to around the woman.

The journal-stealing fiasco had settled her mind on that.

Reaching her room, she decided it was time for a nap. The gray, forbidding weather and the cold called for it, and she thought she might have a late night with Will. The idea filled her with nervousness. She lay down on the bed with no book. She didn't think she would need one as she was still feeling shaky and tired after her ordeal yesterday.

Sleep came for her swiftly as she turned on her side, nestling in for a couple hours. The dream came on at some point—her mother running down the path, sharp stones cutting tender feet. Lillian felt the pain as usual, as if it were her, but tonight, she not only saw her father's face floating above her, pale with worry, but she saw the runner ahead of her as a figure that could only be Samson. He was wearing a pair of jeans, and even in fear, his gait was like that of a graceful antelope. Moonlight gleamed off of his brown, muscular back, and she felt such a longing for him that it scared her. "Hurry, Gretchen," he called in a loud whisper. They ran on, she just a bit behind him, her pale nightgown flapping in the cold wind. She could hear the voices hooting behind her, or was it one voice? She strained to hear, but could not tell with the echoes of the wood surrounding her. A bramble tore at her leg, and she cried out softly. Silence descended, and Samson signaled her to quit running.

"Whoever it was is gone now. I think we're safe—for now, anyway." He reached out and grabbed her in a tight hug, his body wet with sweat against hers. "We'd better head for home another way." He kissed her softly, and she didn't want to move or leave at all, but she knew it was heading on toward morning, and the night had already gone disastrously since someone certainly knew about them and was determined to scare them to death—or worse. Gretchen didn't want to think about that possibility.

They held hands and pressed closely together in the chill as they went down the other dirt path back toward Magnolian—the path that ran parallel to the main one that would have taken them on to the white tower. They could soon see a single light in the window at Magnolian—in the kitchen.

"I love you, Samson." She held him tightly for a moment. "I'll sneak in the back way again. Be careful walking home." She kissed him hard. They finally let go of each other, watching the other walk away until each was just a dark line against a gray-black sky. She saw him cross over and move in front of the water tower path and then across the line of trees that began the forest. She was more worried than she ever had been so far in her young life as she reached the house.

Lillian woke up, sucking in breath. The room was freezing. Her teeth chattered. She looked to her right and saw Samson—more substance than shadow at this point. It seemed his essence was growing stronger as he tried to tell her something.

She reached out a hand for him, and he disintegrated, a look of anguish on his fine features. He was gone, and she woke up unsure of whether it was night or day until she saw the blank gray sky of early dusk.

Chapter 11

Farewell, O Warbler! till to-morrow eve, And you, my friends!
farewell, a short farewell!
We have been loitering long and pleasantly, And now for our dear
homes.
—from "The Nightingale" by William Wordsworth

Still feeling groggy from her disquieting nap, Lillian shambled into the bathroom and brushed her teeth to get the acrid taste of fear out of her mouth. This dream had been different. She had fully inhabited her mother's body—feeling the same things she did. The memory of Samson's sinewy body against hers made her pulse speed up. She smiled a little as she brushed her hair, understanding completely how her mother had fallen in love with Samson. He was like a dark angel with an innocent heart. She had sensed that in their dream run together. She had felt the purity of her mother's love for him—unblemished by judgment or prejudice. Knowing that made her all the more sad for how things had turned out for them.

She slowly put on a coat of foundation, brown mascara, blue eyeliner, a touch of peach blush, and nude lip gloss. She wanted to look nice for her date tonight, but she wasn't sure how nice. She shook her head at herself in the mirror, frowning at her indecision. What was wrong with Will? Dozens of women within a twenty-mile radius would throw themselves at him and rip his clothes off if given half a chance. Why did he seem to want her, if he did, if he could be trusted? She liked him, but she still didn't fully trust his father or him or know her own future. She wasn't willing to give it over to Will yet—if ever.

Smacking her lips together, she turned to her clothes and chose a forest-green long-sleeved tunic, black leggings, and black Mary Janes. Nice but not too sexy. Satisfied, she walked down the hall to tell Grand goodbye.

Grand's door was open, and she was puttering around in her room, organizing her makeup table. Lillian noticed that her huge stack of novels had also been pruned. She definitely got her reading from both sides of the family.

"Grand! I'm so glad you're up and busy. You look great." Lillian grinned at her as they hugged.

And she did. Her hair was perfectly in place, and her makeup looked flawless. The scent of White Shoulders drifted from her general vicinity. Lillian smiled. That fragrance brought back memories of this house and of playing with Grand's makeup as a very young child—in this very room.

"I figured I needed to quit moping around since your young man will be here in a day or so." Grand looked at her. "Didn't forget, did you?" She almost cackled.

"Are you going out with Will tonight?" She smiled a half smile at Lillian. "Oh, I already know the answer. He's a charmer, isn't he?" She smiled at Lillian and lifted her shoulders as if to say, "Oh, well."

"Yes, that he is, but I don't know if I'm charmed. I'm just having dinner at his place. I don't turn down free meals cooked by handsome men since they've been a rare event in my life—up till now, that is." Lillian laughed.

"I know what you mean. I felt that way about your grandfather for a long time. He was slick and handsome, a real ladies man, but I didn't know if he was for me. Turned out he was, but you'll have to find your own way through all of that. You know if it's right. You always do." Grand closed the last drawer on her makeup stand and turned to her. She pecked Lillian on the cheek. "Don't be late, and have a good time. Be careful!" Her face grew stern with that last order, and Lillian wasn't sure if she was referring to being on her guard with Will or watching out for further accidents. Either way, she would take it as sage advice, she thought, turning to go.

"I will. I love you, Grand. See you later tonight or tomorrow." She opened the door to go.

Grand's eyes twinkled like flowers on a sunny day. "It'll be tomorrow, honey, and you know it. Enjoy yourself, but remember what I said about the Tates." Grand frowned and sighed.

Lillian's smile stayed put down the hall and to the end of the staircase. She felt that with this last exchange with Grand, she had received her blessing with Will or with Donovan. It was a good feeling. She frowned, remembering her mother had not been so lucky. How lonely she must have felt, Lillian thought sadly.

She was glad to meet no one else on her way out the front door. She grabbed Percy's keys from the table where he had kindly left them for her again. He had walked on to his home just down the road. A lump built in her throat at the thought of his kindness. What kind of man would his grandson have been if he had only lived? Pushing the somber thought away, she got into the truck, shaking a little in the cold breeze. It seemed that too many ghosts stayed on her shoulder these days, and they all centered around Magnolian. She again had a feeling of freedom as she put the pillars of its entrance in her rear view mirror.

She enjoyed the drive through Everwood. She could really come to love this place, she thought. The main thoroughfare was obviously that of a small town, but it still had plenty of cars darting to and fro and a thriving business section with upscale shops, chic renovated homes now serving as businesses, and a lovely park in its center. She frowned at her line of thinking—best not to get too attached to this place. Things might not work out long term. She turned down a lovely Main Street dotted with splendid old Queen Anne and Georgian style homes. The color white predominated and shone in the night, as did the finely manicured lawns that accompanied such places.

She was looking for 87 Roeville Avenue. "Here it is," she murmured to herself, pulling through a circular drive way to stop in front of a charming gray-and-white-trimmed ranch style home. Will had taste, but his taste wasn't gaudy. The house looked at least fifty years old and was not ostentatious. These things made her like him even more. She could deal with the Mercedes, she guessed, smiling as she thought of it. Her father would have laughed and gotten into a spirited discussion about what cars people should drive and what they say about them. But you're not your father, she told herself, and she knew that was true. She still had to tease out many of her own values for herself.

She slipped out of the truck and made her way to the brightly lit porch. Before she could knock, Will opened the door. She felt temporarily blinded by the porch light on his blond hair. He was illuminated like the sun.

"Hey, hey! You made it." She snapped out of her romantic thoughts with a smile.

He was holding a bottle of champagne that he had obviously already opened, judging from his rosy cheeks and happy demeanor. He was wearing a light-blue off-brand polo shirt with khaki slacks. He knew how to accentuate the positive, Lillian thought with a grin when he turned to lead her into the house. The scent of curry assailed her.

"Is that curry I smell? I hope so." She grinned at him as he stirred something on the stove.

"Yes, it is—my specialty, curried chicken with brown rice and veggies." He smiled as she sat down at the kitchen table, watching him.

"Is there anything I can do to help? I hate just showing up and saying I want to eat." She smiled at him.

"It's all done. Just relax." He hummed a happy tune under his breath as he cooked.

Lillian felt a sense of warmth and safety in that moment that she had longed for in the past months. She had not felt that often with him, so it was a change. She could only blame her distrust on their water-tower debacle and on his father.

"Would you like some champagne or white wine or something else entirely?" he asked, eyebrows raised.

"I'll have what you're having, because you seem happy." Lillian laughed.

He poured her a glass of bubbly pink champagne, and she giggled as the bubbles popped in her nose on the first sip. She would have to watch herself with this stuff. It tasted sweet and went down smoothly.

"Ready to eat? It's done." He served up big helpings of curry, and they sat down at his modern black and silver table. It looked like an IKEA special—nice but not furniture that would blow a budget.

"These plates are lovely," she said, noticing the maroon colored, square bowls they were eating off of.

"Thanks. I made those myself, believe it or not." He beamed at her as he took a bite of curry.

"Wow! A man of so many talents. How long have you been doing this?" She really was impressed. She had not pictured him as a man who would have a calm hobby like pottery. Perhaps he was deeper than she had dreamed.

"Ten years. Practice makes perfect. I mainly just have fun with it, but I sell a piece every now and again." He took a bite of curry.

She had a feeling he was being modest, but that was fine by her. Not enough men could show humility, in her experience.

They ate in silence for a few minutes. "So, Lily girl, what secret hobbies do you have that I haven't heard about? Weaving away in the attic or collecting colorful butterflies? Hmm?" He leaned toward her and ran his hand down her arm, sending a little shock through her.

"Writing. That's it. That's my only deep, dark secret." She felt herself flushing and was annoyed.

She wished she had dark skin or thicker skin in general.

Will laughed softly, and she knew it was at her pink face. "Well, that's not so bad, is it? You have the soul of a writer, I think." He looked at her, and she read his feelings for her in his eyes. Their expression scared her. He joked, but he was not joking about what he had said to her early on when they met.

They cleared off the dishes after a wonderful peach cobbler—homemade from a family recipe—and settled in to watch a movie. He had chosen a light comedy, and Lillian was relieved. She didn't think she could take a ghost story or a love story tonight. Still, he snuggled close to her on the couch, and the heat from his body made her heart trip faster. She focused on the movie as much as possible, but he traced her jawline with his fingertips and reached over to kiss her neck toward the end of it. The male protagonist couldn't hold a candle to him.

When it was over, they sat in silence for a moment. He turned her face to his and kissed her deeply. She felt her body respond. He touched her shoulders lightly, and they lay back on the couch. He stopped kissing her and just held her, sensing that she had stiffened in his arms.

"What is it, Lily? I want you, but I'm willing to wait on you." He caressed her face with his fingertips and kissed her eyelids gently.

She didn't know what to say, so she kissed him again. It was enjoyable, but was it anything more than passion? She wasn't sure. He sat up and put his arm around her.

"Tongue tied, eh?" He tucked her hair back behind her ears. "That's okay. There's no rush. Thanks for letting me get to know you better. I just enjoy being with you. I could sit here with you all night, just looking at you, you know?" The thick pillar candle he had lit shined in his blue eyes, making them glow like water under a setting sun.

"Likewise," she said, nearly speechless, and kissed him again. After a few minutes, they parted with some regret, and he said, "Let's stop there for now. Otherwise, I'm not going to be able to control myself much longer. You're bringing out the beast in me." He winked and grinned at her.

They talked for a while longer about this and that, carefully avoiding ghosts and other talk of Magnolian, and then she decided to call it a night after telling him what she needed to but wished she didn't have to. She had thought about mentioning Donovan to him on and off all night. She decided she must—that it was only fair. If he did care about her, the least she could do was be honest so he wasn't shocked to see her with someone else while Donovan was visiting.

"Before I go, I have to tell you something." She cleared her voice, strained with laughter and other pursuits of the night and looked at him in the flickering candlelight.

"Why so serious? Lay it on me. I can take it." He held her hand in his.

"Well, a friend of mine is coming down in a couple days—on Monday evening. His name is Donovan." She dropped the name like a rock in still water.

Will's face didn't change. "Okay. That's cool. Thanks for letting me know." She could hear the hurt in his tone, but he kept it out of the stony expression he now wore.

"I wanted to tell you—I'm sure you'll meet sometime while he's here. I didn't want things to be awkward." She had expected more from him than this, but she was relieved by his reaction. She hated dramatic scenes, and they had already had their share.

"Hey, it's fine. Seems you do have some secret hobbies after all, Lily. I underestimated you. But hey, you told me 'just friends' days ago. I just didn't want to hear it." His mouth lifted in a half grin. He stood up first as if urging her to leave now.

"Good night. Thanks for everything. I really enjoyed it, Will." She stood close to him by the door, but he didn't lean in to kiss her again.

"Me, too. Take care, Lily girl. I'll be seeing you." He shut the door, and she turned, feeling a bit hurt, but realizing she had no reason to.

She walked outside into the frosty air, her breath puffing white in front of her. She didn't feel happy, but she felt that she had done the right thing in telling Will about Donovan, and she had to admit, she couldn't wait to see him. She spent the drive home thinking about him and humming Bach with a smile on her face.

When she reached Magnolian, the house was dark and quiet, like a brooding white giant. It appeared foreboding at this time of night—eleven o'clock on her glowing watch dial. She parked Percy's truck and got out, noticing the utter silence of the front lawn. To her right, she thought she saw a shadowy shape, but she hurried quickly on, looking straight forward. It was with relief that she unlocked the front door and re-secured the lock firmly behind her. A single lamp was on, so she took care entering the house. She climbed the stairs slowly and carefully. She didn't want any accidents tonight. Tomorrow Grand would want to go to church, and Monday Donovan would be coming to visit. That thought put a smile on her lips even as she realized how tired she was. The bad dreams and other stresses were taking a toll on her.

She peeled her clothes off quickly and fell into bed after brushing her teeth and hurriedly washing her face. Some time near dawn, she woke up—at least partially—aware of a hand on her head, smoothing her hair. The room was as frigid as an igloo. Her teeth chattered, but she didn't want to open her eyes in the still night almost dawn. When she did open them a crack, she saw the spectral image of Samson clearly, standing beside her bed, running his fingers through her hair with a look of such want and craving on his face that it frightened her into rigidity. Through her fear, she felt her body respond, and she moaned with pleasure and terror. She felt so safe when he touched her but so afraid at what he was and who she was. She summoned her strength and bolted upright in bed. His image and form vanished, and the room began to warm up. Lillian whispered, "Samson, I know you are concerned about Gretchen, but Gretchen is dead. She lived a happy life while she had it. I'm Lillian, as you know. I'm okay. You can watch over me if you'd like, but I can't love you like she did."

She settled back down on her pillow, pulling the sheet around her. She couldn't quit shivering for some time.

Somehow, she felt that she was being heard. She knew that Samson was not an entity to be feared. The emotion behind his nightly visits, though, had a power that was barely restrained by the separate spheres they inhabited of life and afterlife. It drained her and made her sad that she had, so far, been unable to help him. She lay back down and managed a couple hours of sleep before the alarm's shrill ring.

Chapter 12

My heart aches, and a drowsy numbness pains my sense, as though of
hemlock I had drunk,
—from "Ode to a Nightingale" by John Keats

Sunday dawned warm and bright with lemon-yellow sunshine making cheerful patches on the carpet in Lillian's bedroom. She stretched and yawned, shutting the alarm off and sighing. She had a feeling that she had made real contact with Samson last night—maybe eased his suffering a bit by speaking to him of Gretchen. How long must it have been before he had heard her name spoken directly to him? She shivered in the sunlight, thinking about how inconsolable he must be to have waited all this time, appearing only now to her. If that was truly the case, she could not fathom his misery.

She took a shower and got dressed in a fitted black corduroy dress, black bead earrings, and red lipstick. Extra blush helped get rid of the bags under her eyes she had due to lack of good sleep, but she didn't put on so much as to appear clownish. A little brown mascara topped off her look.

When she got downstairs, she was surprised to see Grand and Aunt Lorelei at the dining room table eating bacon, eggs, and pancakes. Her stomach growled.

"Dear, I'm so glad you made it up for church." Grand smiled at her, looking lovely in a mint green suit and rose lipstick. She had even outlined her eyes with black eye liner.

"Me, too." She smiled at Grand, hoping no one noticed how tired she must look.

Aunt Lorelei remained silent, putting away a pancake quickly. She wore a russet red cotton dress, ill suited for the cold weather.

After a hearty breakfast but muted conversation, Percy drove the three women to church in the BMW, despite Lillian's protest.

"Miss Lillian, I go to the Baptist Church, too, now. I just sit in the balcony. You're visiting us, and you need to do things the way we do. I mean, let me drive while you enjoy the sunlight and the view. It's a gorgeous day, yes ma'am." Percy looked at her with a touch of defiance across the front seat of the car. He softened the look with a smile.

"Will do. Thanks for the ride. It's wonderful to be able to enjoy the lovely day." And it was. Obviously, Percy enjoyed going to church with Grand. His wife was an invalid, so he had clearly made the choice himself. Lillian understood for the first time how close the two of them were—despite their ages and races and the past.

The Everwood Baptist Church downtown on Main Street was a lovely Greek Revival style with white columns and a formidable set of steps to the sanctuary. The white steeple shone in the bright sunlight, back lit by a periwinkle sky—the likes of which Lillian had rarely seen in Pittsburgh or California for that matter. It was an impossible blue that happened on the sunniest days here in Alabama. She remembered days like it on other visits.

About halfway through the service, Lillian looked to her right and saw Will sitting in a pew near the front of the church with a very attractive woman about his age. She recognized the woman as Monica from her pictures with Will on Facebook. He was engrossed in her, rather than in the sermon, Lillian noted, as his hand lay on the woman's white skirt. When he caught her looking at them, he winked, and her face burned. Damn him. She felt like a fool, thinking he cared that much about her accepting or rejecting his advances. He probably had a new woman lined up every night. Forcing herself to tune in to the sermon, she found comfort in the words about eternal life, but she wasn't sure that she believed everything worked out as the preacher thought it did. She had believed it in the past, but her experience with Samson and her dreams with her father and mother in them made her wonder. And she just wasn't feeling very churchy today because of the lovely Monica and her buddy Will. That was the real problem, she thought, sighing inwardly as Will grabbed Monica's hand and whispered in her ear as they stood up for the closing hymn, "Amazing Grace."

After church, everyone filed out to shake the pastor's hand or stand on the steps and talk. Will strode purposefully over to Lillian and her companions, the beautiful brunette on his arm.

"Hi, Lily, I'd like you to meet a friend of mine. This is Monica. Monica—Lily."

He watched in obvious pleasure as the two women sized each other up and flashed fake smiles.

"So nice to meet you," Monica drawled, making *you* a continuous vowel, much like Amber did, Lillian thought, irritated. Lillian decided then and there she didn't like her.

"And you," she said shortly and walked away. Grand and Aunt Lorelei ambled behind her down the steps. She was pleased with her reaction to Will. The speech about waiting and blah-blah-blah was just that—a pretty speech by an actor. The strange thing was that she thought it was okay with her. At least, her heart was still in one piece.

She asked Grand if she could go on with Percy and let her catch a ride from the pastor. She wanted to talk with him. She didn't tell Grand about what but intimated that it was a personal issue. Grand raised her eyebrows and patted her arm.

"Certainly, child. We'll save you a seat the restaurant, and Percy will come back for you in ten minutes. If you need longer than that, you can make an appointment with Brother Mark during the week."

Lillian smiled and began searching for the pastor. She soon found him at the top of the steps, shaking hands with a smile. His gray hair was perfectly parted, and his suit looked like a special from Dillard's. She decided she liked him. She approached him as the last stragglers shook his hand and walked down the steps.

"Brother Mark, could I speak with you for a few minutes? Right here will be fine. I don't want to take up a lot of your time." She smiled at him. "I'm Lillian Mullins, by the way."

"Of course! I'd heard from your grandmother you'd be in town. So glad to have you." He shook her hand warmly, and turned his megawatt smile on her. His voice was mild and reassuring.

"I have something I want to run by you."

"Sure. Let's go back in the sanctuary, if that's okay with you." They walked back into the warmer sanctuary and sat near the middle with some distance between them on the pew.

"Now, what can I help you with, Lillian?" He looked at her earnestly.

"Do you believe in ghosts, Brother Mark?" She decided not to mince words since time was of the essence.

He looked taken aback. "Not really. I believe once we die, we are dead—until the Resurrection, that is." He smiled at her. "Why? Do you?"

"Yes, I think I do—now. I've seen one several times—for the first time in my life. I don't want to go into too much detail, but I think this spirit is not at rest. I want to help him." She clasped her hands, staring at the light shafting through a stained glass window with the image of Jesus with arms outstretched.

He looked alarmed and cleared his throat, obviously measuring his words. "Well, Lillian. That sounds like a dangerous situation to me. My advice is to cut contact with the spirit. Scripture warns against talking with the dead or seeking to."

"But what if he seeks to talk with me? What if he needs me?" She heard the desperate note in her voice and flushed.

He looked at her for a long moment. "Then there is even more danger to you. Have you considered leaving Magnolian? Your soul may be in the balance."

Lillian was startled. "No, I'm not leaving. He needs my help."

Tears pooled in her eyes.

"All I can suggest is that you pray for him and claim the room for Jesus Christ whenever you encounter the spirit." He splayed his hands in resignation.

She smiled weakly. "I'll do what you suggest. It can't hurt. If it helps him, I'll be happy."

The pastor rose with her and patted her shoulder. "Call me any time. If things get worse, please call. I'll figure something out. I have friends who know more about this sort of thing than I do. The Catholic minister in town is one of them. I think he's had a little experience—not a lot, but more than I've had with exorcisms and the like." He looked away, turning a bit red.

"Okay. I'll keep that in mind. Thanks for your help." They walked down the steps together, and she spotted Percy at the bottom. She didn't plan to contact the Catholic minister. She figured doing what Brother Mark had suggested couldn't hurt. It might even help.

"You ready, Miss Lillian?" Percy asked, his hands at his side.

"I sure am. Let's go." She smiled as they walked to the car.

Percy and the women ate lunch at Joe's Fish House in town. Paddles and captain's wheels served as décor, along with huge fishing nets and gaping fish of all hues. The Gulf grouper with turnip greens was delicious. Lillian decided that she had never had fish until now. On their way out of the restaurant, she saw Joe Tate sitting in a booth with his wife, Mary. She had not met her, but Will had talked about her the night before—her gentle spirit and goodness. She had sounded like, and definitely looked like, a contrast to Joe. She walked up to them to introduce herself to Mary.

"Sorry to interrupt you two. I'm Lillian." She smiled at the other woman.

"Yes, I've heard a bit about you from my two boys." She wiggled her eyebrows, and Lillian laughed.

"I'm Mary, and it's so good to meet you—finally." She grinned, and Lillian could tell she was being sincere. She liked her immediately. She wondered, as she had with other couples, how these two had ever gotten together.

Grand signaled that she, Percy, and Aunt Lorelei would be waiting outside for her. Lillian decided to press her luck.

"So, Joe, did you talk with Mary by any chance about what we discussed in your office yesterday?" She looked at him, unblinking.

Joe put on a blank look, but his eyes glinted. "What do you mean, Lillian?"

"About Samson Jones." She said it outright, challenging his game with a stare.

Mary blanched. "That poor boy. I can't stand to think about him even to this day, and he was never found. Did Joe tell you he helped the search party—tirelessly? How sad it all was." Mary shook her head.

"He did mention something of the sort," Lillian said. Joe really hadn't mentioned it, though. Mary made it sound like he had been one of the main searchers. That would have given him plenty of leeway in covering his tracks or hiding any part he had played in Samson's murder. And Lillian knew it was murder. She smiled at Joe. His face was red with unexpressed emotion. Anger or embarrassment, she wasn't sure.

"It was good to meet you, Mary. I'd best get back to the family." Lillian smiled and half turned to leave.

"I might see you later on, Lillian. I'm heading out to your Grand's this afternoon to help Percy with something." Joe smiled, and she waved and walked out.

Lillian turned the whole thing over in her head on the way home. She was glad Percy had driven because she was too distracted to do so. She went up to her room as soon as they got home and took out a pen and paper. She thought it was time to add to the notes she had begun making a few days before so she wouldn't forget the details she had learned so far. From what she could tell, only Joe had any motive to have Samson gone for good. Grand had mentioned his love of

Magnolian and how he allied himself with the family, distant relation that he was. The money and name of the family would have been tarnished if a love affair between Gretchen and a black man had come out. The family would have been ostracized or at least whispered about and shunned politely. Such ties would have spelled disaster for the mayoral campaign and office that Joe Tate had been running for and had held at the time. To have anything come to light after all these years could ruin an even bigger prize, that of the office of governor of the state of Alabama. She was not sure she believed it, as well as it worked out, though.

Lillian stowed her notes away in her night stand drawer, under the journal. She would have to keep digging for more information or something incriminating. Right now, she had nothing, and Samson's spirit wasn't going anywhere, nor, she assumed, was the person who had tried to hurt or kill her twice.

Lillian lay down on the bed and fell asleep. She awoke, feeling refreshed, as shadows slanted through the blinds. She decided to fire up her laptop and transfer her notes there so she could destroy the hard copy of them. This took her some time, as did checking her email. She was happy to find a return email from the prospective internship assuring her that March would be fine as a start date.

A quiet knock sounded on the door. She stowed her laptop and opened the door a crack. It was Leticia bearing a tray of cold lunch meat and a cup of tea.

"That looks heavenly. Thanks so much. Sorry I didn't make it down for dinner. I got busy napping and doing other stuff."

Leticia smiled and left. It was after eight, and they must have had dinner without her, or more likely Grand didn't make it down for dinner. She was probably fatigued after church.

Lillian ate with relish, not leaving a scrap of her sandwich or pecan pie on the plate. She swallowed her tea, enjoying the warmth as it went down. Soon after, she began to feel funny. At first, she felt so tired she could barely sit up. Then she wanted to throw up. It occurred to her that something she ate had made her ill. Then, with alarm, she realized that her breathing was changing. Something had been in her food. She stumbled to her door and threw it open. She yelled in the hallway, at the top of the landing, a garbled call for help. She managed to stagger down the steps, holding tight to the railing. Bile rose in her throat.

"Ahhhhh," she said, the sound not coming out like the scream she meant it to. Only one long syllable came out.

Before everything went black, she saw Percy running toward her.

When she came to, a crowd of faces overlooked her—Percy, Grand, and Leticia. She was tucked in to her bed. A kind looking man with silver hair and bushy gray brows was examining her by poking and prodding.

"Lillian, does anything hurt? Nod if you can't talk. Your throat might hurt from the vomiting."

He touched her stomach and pressed.

"Just my head and my throat," she rasped.

"Well, you vomited up most of whatever it was. I'm guessing a couple grams of morphine. If it had been another gram more, you might not be with us, young lady. Someone wanted to scare you badly."

"What? Someone poisoned me?" Lillian's head was spinning.

"Yes, that's what I'm saying." The doctor's face was serious as he finished poking and prodding her and pulled the sheet over her.

Grand's eyes were huge. "But why? Why would anyone..." Her voice was reedy, and the doctor looked at her with worry.

"Percy, could you take Beverly to her room?"

Percy nodded and then asked, "Do you think we should report this to the police, Dr. Smythe? Or could it have been an accident?"

Dr. Smythe shook his head. "It was no accident. Making it a police matter is up to you. I suggest whatever grievances you all have with each other in this house—you need to make peace and talk it out before something worse happens. I won't report it to anyone this time unless Lillian wants. What do you say, Lillian?" He looked at her sharply, his hands folded over each other.

"No, please don't. It was probably a prank. I think I know who did it." She tried to smile and make her voice light, but it didn't work.

"It was no prank. You stay safe, young lady, and if you need anything, contact me. Rest for a while and have liquids for the next twenty-four hours. That will help soothe your stomach. You should be feeling better by tomorrow." He gave Percy an unreadable look. "Please look after her, Percy." Percy mumbled that he would.

"Percy, don't take me to my room. I need to stay with Lillian!" Grand protested with a mewl.

"I'm okay, Grand." She managed a half smile despite the pain in her stomach.

"All right, dear. I love you. I'll check on you in the morning." Grand shuffled out with Percy supporting her.

The doctor looked worried as he patted her on the arm. "All right, young lady, you've had a close brush today. I want you to take it easy tonight, and watch what you eat. Either make it yourself, or have Leticia do it. I'd trust her with my life. The others here—I don't know. I wish I did, but I'm being perfectly honest with you." He rose from the bedside. "Get some sleep. If you need anything, I can come back. Don't hesitate to call."

"I'll call if I need anything. Thanks again. Doc?" Her voice rose because she couldn't remember his name and didn't know if she ever had known it.

"Doc Smythe," he said with a tight smile. "Bye now."

"Oh, Doc? Lock that door on your way out—if you don't mind." He looked at her for a long moment and locked the door as he pulled it closed behind him.

Lillian collapsed back against the bed, tears falling on her pillow. She felt alone and scared, though she knew she wasn't alone. She trusted Grand, didn't she? Her head was spinning. She honestly didn't know whom she could trust anymore. Someone had poisoned her—

come very close to killing her. It could have been anyone—Joe Tate had said he would be coming by today. Aunt Lorelei—and where was she anyway during the excitement? Even Grand or Percy. Like Doc Smythe, she trusted Leticia. She had seen her love for her mother a few days ago, and she had felt in her gut that it was real.

She decided to quit puzzling it all over and try to get some sleep. It was past nine, and Donovan would be here tomorrow afternoon if his flight was on time. As she was drifting off, she heard a tapping on the door.

"Who is it?" Her voice sounded strained, even to her ears.

"Aunt Lorelei. Let me in. I need to talk to you." Her voice was strident.

Lillian sighed and pulled herself slowly out of bed, walking stiffly to the door.

"Yes?" She opened the door and turned back toward the bed.

Aunt Lorelei padded across the room to her bedside. "How are you?" She asked, looking sharply at Lillian. She smoothed out her bright yellow floor length house dress and sat at the end of Lillian's bed, studying her with a wrinkled up nose, as if she smelled.

"Better now, but still not great. I don't know when I'll be great again." She smoothed her pillow out and lay back.

"I just wanted to check on you. Glad you're all right. If you need anything in the night, just holler." Lorelei smiled, but it looked more like a grimace.

"All right, thanks. I appreciate that." Lillian sank down in the bed. "Oh, and lock the door as you leave, please." Her cheeks flamed as she said this, but there was no way she was leaving it unlocked tonight.

Wordlessly, her aunt locked the door. Once her footsteps faded in the hall, Lillian crept across the room to check the door. It was locked. She sighed in relief that no one would be getting in tonight.

Her sleep was a deep blank—dreamless. She was so tired she forgot to pray a blessing over the room as Brother Mark had suggested. That night, it didn't seem to hurt that she had forgotten.

The sun spotting the window and dazzling her with its brightness roused her in the morning. The day looked warm and inviting, and she smiled, thinking that Donovan would be here in a few hours. Before he arrived, she had things to do, but she would have to move slowly. She ached all over, probably from vomiting and passing out on the stairs.

She went down and had a quick breakfast of chicken noodle soup and watered-down juice. She felt babyish, but the food hit the spot. Her appetite was a little off, but she managed fine and kept her food down. Everyone made a stop in the dining room to ask about her, and they all seemed relieved that she was feeling better. After breakfast, she checked with Leticia to see which bedroom Donovan would have during his stay. She was happy to learn it was the one right next door. Grand obviously didn't hold with keeping young folks separated as far apart as possible. Lillian had always had the inkling that Grand wasn't as old-fashioned as some.

Lillian spent the morning in the bedroom set for Donovan to use. She told Leticia she would make sure it was ready for him and to take a break. Leticia gave her a grumpy look at first, but then smiled and sat down with a cup of tea in the dining room. Moving slowly, Lillian aired out the bed, shook out the pillows, dusted, vacuumed, and generally straightened the room up. It looked like it had been in long disuse, though its palette of navy blue and teal with white carpet was lovely and masculine. She was exhausted by the time she was done.

She decided to take a nap before Donovan would arrive. She didn't want to be dragging like she was when he got there. The nap refreshed her tremendously, and she felt like her old self when she woke up at one o'clock and had a quick lunch of soup and pears. Donovan called from the airport at two o'clock to say he had arrived and was on his way. It would only be an hour or so now.

Lillian couldn't help herself when he drove up in a tan Toyota Yaris. She had told herself she was going to play it cool, but she ran out of the house into the balmy air that told tales of spring rather than the middle of autumn and leaped into Donovan's arms the moment he got out of the car.

"If I had known this would be my reception, I would have been here weeks ago." Donovan laughed, and for the first time, she noticed a dimple in his right cheek. She smoothed his black hair down and looked into his eyes—clear pools of sea green today.

"I'm so glad you're here. You have no idea. Come on, let's get your stuff in." They opened his trunk to unload it.

At that moment, Percy arrived to take the bag upstairs. Donovan thanked him heartily, and the two began talking about fixing cars and other topics. Lillian smiled to see the easy way that the two related.

Back inside, a curious crowd had gathered, all of them trying to appear busy. Grand marched up to Donovan and hugged him warmly while Aunt Lorelei simply nodded as Lillian introduced him. Leticia introduced herself with a brisk "Hello" on the way to cleaning Grand's bedroom as she did twice a week.

They got Donovan's one suitcase upstairs—he was a light packer. Then Lillian suggested they go for a walk. She didn't want to tell him all she had to say in the house where there were eavesdroppers.

"I'd love to. This place is gorgeous. We don't have places like this in Pittsburgh, you know?" Donovan grinned.

"I know what you mean, I think, but be nice. Let's go, but I'm going to have to take it a little slow today. I'm just warning you."

"Oh, why?" A worried look marred his face.

"Well, let me tell you what happened." She told him about the poison incident and said she would tell him the rest when they got there. He was shocked into silence, but he put her arm in his as they walked, as if protecting her. She saw him glance back at Magnolian a couple times as she told him what had happened. Lillian led him on toward the water tower path. She wanted to get away from the house to talk, and that seemed the best place to do it.

They walked along the path, sunlight filtering in on them as they held hands. After a couple minutes, the silence grew, encroaching on the bird songs and rustling of small insects and animals in the brush.

"Do you feel that? It's spooky out here." Donovan stopped and looked at Lillian, green eyes reflecting the forest.

"What do you mean?" But she knew what he was talking about. Her heart tripped faster in her chest. Someone was finally experiencing the same feelings she had had!

"How still and, well, and wrong it is out here suddenly—like someone or something is watching us, but it doesn't feel malevolent, not really. It feels hopeless." He shivered and pulled her close to him, her chin against his thermal shirt.

"I do feel it, and that's what I want to talk to you about. Let's walk a little further." They walked until they came out by the water tower.

"What a spooky place," Donovan almost whispered, looking around as if in awe.

She clutched his hand tightly as they sat in the grass. "I'm going to tell you about something you won't believe." She took a deep breath and launched into her story, the stillness pressing in around them. He interrupted her a dozen times, making sure she meant what she said or asking her to clarify part of the story. When she was done, he just looked at her, mouth hanging open a little.

"It sounds so crazy, but I feel what you feel out here. I can believe you. I mean, I do believe you. I can't believe I'm saying that, but I believe you. Maybe you won't feel so alone now. I can't imagine what all of this must have been like for you." He pulled her to his chest as a twig popped here and there under a bird's feet.

Crying a little, she said, "Thank God. I've been so lonely these last few weeks. There is not one person here I can trust enough to tell them all of this. Well, I have told Will, but that's it. And he doesn't feel the things you do."

"Will?" Donovan looked at her with a raised brow.

"Oh, he's my third cousin." Lillian felt flustered and dishonest.

"I see. Good. I'm glad he's listened to you even if he didn't feel it. If he had, he'd be a believer for sure." He frowned and his mouth set in a line. "We'll find out who's trying to get rid of you—scare you or kill you. I think in the process, we can set Samson free from this dimension, anyway. Wow, that sounds like a sci-fi flick." He laughed, but there wasn't any conviction behind it. They sat by the water tower at the head of the path for hours, talking, but they came no closer to figuring out what to do than they had been when they arrived in the woods.

Chapter 13

Our song is the voice of desire, that haunts our dreams...
—from "Nightingales" by Robert Bridges

As the afternoon died out, losing its bright light, they made their way back down the path. Critters shuffled in the underbrush, and a woodpecker tapped on a nearby tree. The haunting silence had lifted, at least for now. They stopped in the middle of the path to kiss—a slow, lingering kiss that made Lillian's legs turn wobbly. She realized how much she had missed Donovan while they were apart. She also wondered why he could feel the things she felt—the atmosphere of the woods behind Magnolian—while others could not. Perhaps it was his sensitivity to beauty and pain. She had sensed that in him when he played the classics, and she had found it to be true the day he came to her father's funeral. He, like Lillian herself, saw things others missed.

Trying to shift the tone to a lighter one, she asked, "So, are you glad to get a break from the church and everything?" She linked her hand back in his as they walked along.

"Well, yes and no. Things are a little rocky there right now. The Christmas musical is not going well. I hope I can keep my job. I don't know what I'm going to do if I lose it." He ran his fingers through his shiny dark hair.

"What do you mean? They'd be crazy to get rid of you! There's no one else to replace you. People with your many gifts are hard to come by. If they do something like that, I know you can find other work. You're that talented." She smiled and touched his arm as they sauntered on.

"I know you're a fan of mine, and you might think so, but Mrs. Gilroy and Mr. Patten don't think so. They're two old troublemakers, but when they've made trouble in the past, they always got away with it, and the person they made the trouble for was out." He sighed, his mouth in a hard set line. "But I'll stay until they throw me out, if that's what happens. I need this job to make it through graduate school. I have another year and a half left, and I'm not going to leave Pittsburgh. I love it there."

Lillian felt a twinge at his words. "Really? Do you mean you'll never leave, or you won't leave until you're done with school?"

He laughed. "I don't mean never, but I do plan to stay for a while. I love the weather there—the snow and ice and the turning of the leaves we just had. It's like paradise to me. I guess I was made for it, though I never would have known that if I hadn't ended up with my uncle." He smiled sadly, and she thought of his great loss again. Her chest hurt for a minute, thinking of his parents and of her father.

They came out at the end of the path and could see Magnolian through the overhanging limbs in front of them.

"Hey, c'mon, you don't think Alabama is lovely, too?" She asked only part jokingly, and she could hear the querulous tone in her voice, like that of a small child who has not gotten its candy.

"I certainly do. It's gorgeous! And the temperature. Wow. I just think I might not be a Southerner. I don't know if this place takes kindly to interlopers. What do you think?" He looked at her, his face showing that he wasn't playing around.

"That's a good question. Honestly, I don't know. I have been welcomed here, but then maybe that's because I am from here. And my family has money. It's an old family—the Starks." His words troubled her more than she wanted to let on.

"Well, who knows? Maybe the place will really grow on me while I'm here, and maybe I'll be accepted as a true son of the South." He tried and failed for an authentic Southern accent on the last phrase. They cracked up with laughter as they walked around the house to the front.

"Yeah, maybe. Don't think you'll be accepted with that shoddy accent, though." She was still giggling.

"You're not thinking of staying here for good, are you, Lillian?" Donovan looked straight at her as they stopped near the porch, suddenly serious.

"I don't know. I might be. I miss some things about Pittsburgh, but I love it here, too. It feels like a new start even with all the craziness that's going on right now."

"A new start, huh?" Donovan's face grew dark. She knew she had hurt him somehow.

"Donovan, wait. I didn't mean that like it sounded. I want you in the new start. You are in it. You're here." She reached up and kissed him until he believed her.

"Okay, okay. I'm convinced." He smiled slightly, but his eyes were serious.

Dinner was a lighthearted event. Everyone seemed glad to forget, if temporarily, the scary happenings of the past few days and enjoy themselves. Donovan got along with Grand famously. Before Grand went upstairs for the evening, she whispered in Lillian's ear, "You'd better snag that young man. He's a real catch." Lillian smiled and winked at Donovan. Getting the gist of the exchange, he laughed, and they held hands under the table.

He and Percy had hit it off earlier, and Percy made a point to come by the house right after dinner to talk further with him. Donovan's praise of Leticia's cooking after the meal made the stern woman grin for the first time Lillian could remember since she had seen her with Will. Maybe that was it. Leticia just liked good-looking young men. Well, that would make sense, anyway, Lillian thought, stifling a giggle at her musings. Only Aunt Lorelei excused herself from dinner early with a frown, saying she had to go to the store for some more knitting supplies.

They went into the living room to watch a little television before bed.

Donovan looked at her as they sat close together on the couch. "You know, that cooking might change my mind about the South. That was the best fried chicken I've ever tasted, and wow. That sweet tea was amazing." They nestled together on the faded rose patterned sofa.

"That's part of the master plan." Lillian giggled. She spoke in an overdone Southern accent. "Many a fine Yankee man has been slain by the cooking of the South."

He stopped her giggling with a kiss that made her gasp. She felt such tenderness and passion for him in that moment. She wasn't sure if she had ever felt the two combined that way. She stroked his face, feeling the smooth planes of it and the coil of desire in her stomach. He trailed his long fingers down her neck, and she shivered. They reluctantly pulled themselves apart. The timing wasn't right for anything more, and she was so unsure of everything with regard to Will and Donovan. She decided to enjoy being with Donovan, without thinking about the complications. They sat together for a while after the movie they had been watching went off. In the wee hours of morning, they got up and walked quietly up the stairs. Outside her door, Donovan kissed her. "I'll be thinking only of you until morning. If you need anything, yell. I'll be right there," he said with a smile.

She touched his lips with her fingers and turned toward her room, half wishing he would follow her. She locked her door, smiling at the thought that he could not get in even if she wanted him to, but neither could whoever meant her harm.

Even though it was late, Lillian was keyed up, thinking about Donovan and his being right next door. For a while, she listened to every rustle. Soon, she heard light snoring from his side of the wall. She decided to try to do the same and quiet her mind. Pulling the lamp switch, she plunged the room into darkness.

Sometime during the night, she realized she was dreaming. She was herself and not herself. She felt somehow younger and more daring with skin that didn't feel quite like her own. She was seeing Magnolian and life through her mother's eyes again.

She walked behind the house, not much changed from the way it was now other than that the garden was well tended, and ivy vines climbed the back of the house. The weather was hot, and she was wearing bell-bottom jeans and a peasant blouse. She pulled her hair up into a quick ponytail as she headed near the mouth of the water tower path. Her hair was longer now—long like her mother's had been because she was her mother. She knew he would be there clearing some of the trees and wood out of the way. She was going to talk to him today. Her breath came fast as she saw him from a distance—wearing a white shirt and dark jeans. His actions were quick and economical as he chopped at a long branch at the head of the trail. As full of determination as she was to talk to him, she was also afraid of being seen or caught out. But if anyone did see her, what would they think? She was just the darling of the family talking to a servant about something—like the best ways to clear a trail or how to use scrap wood. The idea of her being in love with Samson, a black man who worked on the estate, was so out of the question that no one would ever suspect. Would they? She had heard of one such case at her school, but these things were done away from parents' eyes in the neighborhoods of the poor. If the rich or upper middle class were involved, they hid their doings and still married as they were expected to with most people none the wiser.

Besides, she had gone on a date with Jack Buck, a pimply-faced, bull-bodied senior who had been bugging her to go out with him all year, last weekend and let everyone know it. She wanted them to think she was interested in him to throw any suspicion away from the true object of her affections. Her feigned interest couldn't be further from the truth. He bored her with his constant talk of football and beer—and occasionally the weed he smoked after school and had offered her once. She had better things to do with her life than hook up with any of the Jack Buck type men of Everwood, but to the eyes of those would who care, he was a perfectly acceptable young man from the Bucks family—a wealthy family that had been in Everwood since its inception. She smiled a bit to think of how she was pulling one over on so many snooty people.

She certainly hadn't shown Jack any interest beside polite talk. When he had taken her parking and kissed her, shoving his hands down the front of her blouse as he sucked at her lips, she had pulled away as if singed by fire. Softening her rejection of him, she had played the inexperienced-for-now but maybe-later-willing girl. That had kept him on the string, and they had another date for this weekend that she was dreading. She felt bad about leading him on in a small way, but it was to protect Samson. No one could know about her feelings for him—at least not now. He hadn't returned her love yet anyway, but that was going to change starting today. She was only a few yards from him now, and her heart skipped in her chest as she looked at his profile—like that of a Roman god. His classical features of planes and clean lines made her weak. She might be inexperienced with men, but she sensed that what he made her feel was as old as time itself.

He looked up, startled as he heard the pine cones crunch under her feet near him.

"Hello, Miss, um, Miss Gretchen. Can I help you with something?" He looked at her with impossibly dark fringed brown eyes. She could see her reflection in them as she stared back at him, a challenge in her eyes.

"No. I just want to talk to you. How are you?" She smiled at him..

He looked even more shocked. "I'm okay. Doing great actually. Just getting some exercise clearing out some brush. It's mighty overgrown back here." He picked up his shears.

"Oh, I was hoping we might talk for a minute—if you can take a break, I mean." She tapped her toe unconsciously, impatient to be with him, to talk with him further.

He was totally still now, gauging her with a slight frown.

"Excuse me, but what could you and I possibly have to talk about?" His face was hard, and his expression darkened.

"A lot, I think. I want to find out, Samson." Her voice softened as she spoke his name, and she saw his eyes open wide. "I want to meet you here on Thursday afternoon—near the water tower, after you're done. Would anyone miss you?"

His jaw dropped, and he quickly shut his mouth. "No, not that I know of. I can just tell them I had to walk down the road for something—that is, if I come." He flushed under his dark skin.

"Good. Okay, I'll see you next Thursday then. I'll find you near the water tower late afternoon."

She turned and left in a swish of fluttering sleeves, already thinking about their meeting in a few days.

Samson dropped his ax, watching her walk away. He wondered if she had seen him looking at her from the corner of his eye, every chance he got, thinking he could never talk to her other than in a passing hello. Perhaps she was teasing or taunting him. That had to be it—playing the lady of the manor, was she? He smacked into the tree with the shears—hard, his anger building. Gretchen Stark would find out he was no fool if it was a game she was playing. He would make sure of that. He was no one's servant boy to be toyed with by the mistress of the plantation. Nothing else made sense to him. There was no way she could actually be interested in knowing him. Could she? Lost in his thoughts, he hacked away at the overgrowth around the trail head.

Lillian woke up with a start, realizing where she was—in bed in her own body and in her own room. The dream had been so real and exhausting. She had walked and talked through it all and felt the intense love and longings of Gretchen and Samson via Gretchen's intuition and through what she saw and felt after Gretchen had gone back to the house. Her head was pounding. It seemed her dreams were going backward. She wondered why she was seeing the start of the love affair through her mother's eyes. She knew that that was what she was seeing—not something she herself was inventing based upon journal entries—but the real words, feelings, and actions of the two lovers.

She sighed and drew the covers around her, sleeping until the sun came up anemically like a child's pen flashlight rays shining behind a gray piece of paper. Lillian felt like she hadn't slept at all, and she wondered how long these dreams could go on. She was physically drained, and it occurred to her that she might be damaging her health. She put her head in her hands. No matter what, she would see it through to free Samson from his earthly chains and see justice for the monster who had destroyed the lives of him and her mother. She felt a bit more positive in her thinking today. After all, there were a few people who had heard her out and who were on her side. Donovan was one of them, she thought with a slow smile as she slid out of bed, stretching like a lithe animal.

She showered in the hottest water she could stand to help her wake up and feel human again and applied her makeup carefully, using concealer around the dark rings under her eyes. She wasn't prone to them, and she knew that the dream and the stress of the whole affair had brought them on. Being poisoned certainly could not have helped. Applying pink lipstick to her mouth and light pink blush, she thought she looked less like a day-old corpse and more like a fresh dead body. Wiggling her nose in distaste at her image in the mirror, she brushed her hair and headed out of the room to wake up Donovan. She smiled to herself at the task. He was still snoring. She knew just the thing to wake him up, she thought with a soundless laugh.

Chapter 14

Alone, aloud in the raptured ear of men we pour our dark nocturnal secret...
—from "Nightingales" by Robert Bridges

A groggy but smiling Donovan pushed her out of the room a few minutes later so he could shower and meet her downstairs for breakfast. The house was quiet. She sat alone at the table over oatmeal and bacon.

Grand shuffled down the stairs and sat across from her, violet eyes shining. She was looking better and better these days, Lillian thought, while Lillian looked worse. Something about the idea nagged at her. She wondered if Grand was as sick as she had let on. Then she brushed the thought away. Of course she was. She had fainted dead away in her room due to how ill she was. Lillian realized that paranoia was causing her to suspect everyone around here of not being as they appeared.

"Dear, I was thinking, Thanksgiving is just two days away. What special dishes do you want to have this year? Leticia will do a turkey, Southern dressing—none of that Yankee stuff for us unless you just must have your own pan—sweet potato casserole, Parker House roles, and broccoli. Does that sound good?" Grand looked at her expectantly.

"Oh, of course. That sounds wonderful. I can't wait." Even as she said the words, Lillian felt her heart drop. Last Thanksgiving with her father had been a joyous event. He was reveling in his new job and was especially happy frying the turkey and helping her make the special dishes they loved. He had invited two colleagues over, and they had eaten turkey and dressing, watching the snow fall silently outside the dining room window. The holidays were going to be hard this year, and all the complications at Magnolian were just adding to her grief. She sighed.

"Dear? Are you all right? You looked like you were a thousand miles away just then," Grand said with a frown, eating a bite of oatmeal.

"Oh, I'm fine, Grand. Just thinking about Thanksgiving last year. I think the holidays are going to be tough for me this year. I'm so glad I have you and—everyone else." She had avoided naming Donovan or even Will—both of whom had been such good friends and rocks in her life over the past few weeks.

"I know, dear, and I'm so glad to have you in my life. We'll make it a good year this year, but of course you'll miss your father. He was a wonderful man. I'm so glad my Gretchen and you were blessed with him." Grand patted her hand and rose with a sigh. "I'm tired today, so I'm going back up to my room. If you need anything, don't hesitate to come see me, or just come see me even if you don't need anything but just want to talk. Oh. You look pale. Did you sleep okay last night?" Grand asked, taking a second glance at her face.

"I slept just fine. I think I've had a lot of excitement lately. That's all." Lillian smiled in what she hoped was a convincing way.

"That you have, my dear. All right, then. I'll see you later." Grand walked slowly to the steps and clung to them for support the whole way up, making little noises of effort.

Lillian felt ashamed of herself. How could she have possibly thought that Grand's health was better than it seemed? She was obviously doing poorly with only brief intervals of feeling good. Lillian drank her coffee slowly, watching Donovan descend the steps after helping Grand to her room. He was a sight to behold with his still-wet, shiny hair clinging to his head and his wide smile greeting her. Dressed in khaki slacks and a red knit pullover, he looked good enough to eat. Coming around to her, he kissed her head.

"And how did you sleep, Princess?" He ran his fingers through her hair.

"Not so well. Would you believe it?" she said, not wanting anyone to hear them. She took a strip of bacon and popped it into her mouth.

"Oh? More dreams?" His tone was light as he grabbed a bowl of oatmeal and a heap of bacon from the sideboard and poured a big mug of black coffee. She knew he was worried.

"Yes, but this was a really strange one. This dream went back to the first time Gretchen approached Samson." She broke off as the kitchen door swung open and Percy walked in. He gave her a hard look, and she knew he had heard his son's name spoken. She wondered how he could contain himself like he did—how he could keep from asking her about why she had spoken the name. The man was an enigma.

"Hi, Percy," Donovan said smoothly through the tension. "How's your day looking?" He ate a big spoonful of oatmeal.

Percy's face relaxed into a small smile. "Pretty good so far. Not much going on but getting the turkey defrosted today. What could be wrong two days before Thanksgiving anyway? I got so much to be thankful for." He grinned as he grabbed a plate of bacon and a cup of coffee with extra cream and sugar.

"Not much could be wrong. I agree with you," Donovan said, sipping his coffee. "Percy, could I shadow you some this morning, just see what you do out here every day? It's a lovely place, and I'd like to see more of it. I think you'd be the one to show me, right? I mean, if you're willing to put up with me following you around and asking a million questions." Donovan spread his hands in a humble gesture.

Lillian looked sharply at Donovan. She wasn't sure what he was playing at, but she had an idea. She was impressed with his ingenuity.

"That sounds okay. Even better than okay for me to have some company today, if you're sure Miz Lillian won't mind?" Percy swallowed a gulp of coffee and stood up.

"Nah, she's going shopping and stuff anyway, aren't you?" He grinned at her.

"Yep, somebody has to get everything on Leticia's long list. I think she left it here on the table just for me." Lillian picked it up with a grin. "Sounds like a good plan to me." She swallowed the last of her coffee as the men moved toward the door.

"All right, see you later," Donovan said and winked at her behind Percy's back. They walked outside into the gray cold. Lillian shivered in the wake of the cold air and wondered what Donovan was up to. He was obviously going to try to get information from Percy or get a good look around the place. She wasn't sure which, but either sounded like a good idea to her. Percy might be more likely to confide something in him or let something slip that he wouldn't otherwise with her or someone else from the house.

Lillian finished her stack of bacon and her last sips of coffee. She grabbed her purse, a shopping list from Leticia, and Grand's keys to the repaired Camry. She wasn't thrilled about driving the car again, but she knew that was just silly. Only an idiot would rig something to fail twice in a row. No, her enemy was smarter than that, employing three different methods to hurt or scare her. She thought *enemy* and then realized it could be *enemies*. The idea made her frown as she walked out into the gray murky day. The cold sent a shiver through her, and the fog hanging over the skeletal trees didn't improve her mood.

She rolled out of the driveway slowly due to the bad visibility of the morning, the thin branches of empty trees hanging over her as if in futile protection. She hoped tomorrow would be sunny. "If there was no sun, at least there should be snow" had always been her motto. It was highly unlikely the latter was going to happen down here—at least not this time of year. Snow would be most likely in January, if it was going to come at all.

After a slow drive through town, her first stop was the Piggly

Wiggly that happened to be next to Will's office, and she found the long list of groceries she needed. She got the last cart they had and walked out, pushing it through the chilly parking lot. The wind was howling now and didn't bode well for a pretty Thanksgiving. She sank deeper into her gray coat as her ears froze.

As she got into her car, she heard a call, "Hey, pretty lady!" Will jogged over to her car as she saw a couple curious old ladies smiling at him.

"Hi, stranger. All set for tomorrow now?" He smiled at her, looking perfect in a white sweater and black slacks.

"Yeah, think so. It was a madhouse in there. I'll never wait until the last minute to do holiday grocery shopping again. Whew." She mopped her brow where sweat had beaded, realizing that in years past, her father had been there to do the shopping for her. A shadow passed over her mind as she thought again about not having him with her this year.

"So, what did you think of Monica, and how is your guest doing?" Will looked at her like the cat that ate the canary, hands in his pockets as he rocked back on his heels. She didn't like that look, and she wondered what he was plotting.

She smiled until her face hurt. "Monica is lovely, and my guest is fine. Why do you ask?" She arched one brow at him and continued with loading her groceries into the trunk. He moved closer to her.

"Because I'm a nice guy, and I wanted you to like Monica. Why do you think I would ask?" She saw a flicker of anger in his expression.

"Look, Will. I'm not playing games here. I told you from the start that I was in this for friendship. I have too much going on in my life to commit to you or anyone right now. You seemed okay with that or willing to wait and see. Last Saturday night, things probably went too far. I apologize, but I still enjoyed it." She looked up from the trunk where she had placed the last bag and smiled, looking directly into his big blue eyes. She wasn't sorry for what had happened. That was true.

She didn't think he was either.

"Me, too. Hell, I can't stay mad at you for long. Plus, we'll be spending the holiday together tomorrow." He grinned at her.

"What?" She slammed the trunk hatch down.

"Don't sound so excited," he teased, coming closer to her as she walked around to her door and went to open it. "I'll be bringing Monica, so don't worry about me pining away for you while you feed Loverboy grapes."

She groaned. "Okay. I'll see you two there, then. I'm sure you have a turkey or something to stuff now." She turned away, but he pinned her against the inside of the car with his legs against hers and his hands around her arms, between her car and the next one over. Her heart beat furiously in her chest. She hated the effect that he had on her. It was purely physical, she realized. He spelled trouble for her because she liked how reckless he was. She, who had always been a good girl, never pushing the limits as it seemed he did in everything.

He was breathing harshly as he leaned in to kiss her. He bit her lip gently and then kissed her until she almost could take no more.

"Stop! You've proven your point. I find you irresistible." She laughed to cover her excitement and confusion.

He unpinned her, his pale eyes burning like blue fire. "Good. That's all I wanted to know." He turned and walked away, calling , "See you tomorrow!"

Frustration flamed inside of her. What was he doing? Did he want her or not, or was she just a plaything, and why did she even care?

She drove home in a bad mood under a lowering sky. It looked like cold rain was coming just in time for Thanksgiving. After she parked the car, she unloaded the groceries, making a few trips. The house was quiet. Donovan must still be out with Percy, she thought. She found herself relieved for time to think before he got back. She hated the effect that Will had on her—like she couldn't get him out of her mind.

Donovan came in through the front door as she sat at the kitchen table, chin in her hands, staring into space. He stamped his feet and shivered. "Whew, it's nasty out there."

She felt guilty for what had happened with Will. Then she wondered why she should feel guilty. She hadn't been the one to encourage him this afternoon.

"Hi," she smiled and took his cold hand in hers, rubbing it. "Anything to report?"

"Let's go upstairs, and I'll tell you." He kissed her nose, and they tromped up the stairs to her room.

She shut the door quickly. "Well, what happened?"

"Nothing really. I couldn't get Percy to talk about his son, and no one else we ran into today did either. It's like it never happened or like Percy doesn't want to rehash it. One disturbing thing or person, I guess I should say. We ran into Timmy, and he helped Percy out with sorting some things in the shed. He's quite a spooky character. He didn't seem to want to talk with me either."

"Maybe he doesn't. Maybe he's shy." She flipped her hair out of her eyes as they sat on the bed.

"I was thinking, though, that a guy like him would be perfect to do someone's dirty work, as long as it was someone he was afraid of." Donovan looked thoughtful.

"I see what you mean. I've only seen Timmy a couple times. He's really good at staying out of sight." She sighed.

"I know what you mean. I had no chance to talk with him, and believe me, I tried. My feeling, though, is that he's scared of something or of someone." Donovan touched her face.

"It's plausible. I guess we can just keep an eye on him the best we can for now."

"Anyway, I feel like it was a big washout, but I tried." He smiled at her.

"I appreciate it, too."

"Hey, I have an idea." Donovan said, brushing her hair back from her forehead with a gentle touch.

"Yeah?"

"Let's go out for dinner tonight. I think we both need to get away from here for a while." He kissed her on the tip of her nose. "Is that a plan? I could kill for some pizza right now."

"It's a plan because I could, too. Let me go tell Grand before we go. Back in a jiff." She kissed him quickly on the cheek and hopped up off the bed, darting down the hall.

Grand should be up from her nap by now, she thought. She knocked on the door and heard nothing, so she opened it slowly and walked in. No one was there, and the bed was made. "Hmm," she mused aloud. "That's funny." She shrugged her shoulders and walked out after finding a pen and scratch paper to leave a quick note on the dresser.

She popped her head into Donovan's room. "Let's go. I'm starving."

"You're the boss." They walked downstairs and out into the cold grayness, arm in arm. The fog was settling back over the treetops again.

The car warmed up quickly, and they enjoyed the drive through town to the other side, where the Pizza Palace was. The food was surprisingly good for a small, local place, and the cheery colored lights hanging from the ceiling were a nice touch, especially on a night like this one.

"So, are you still glad you came?" She smiled at Donovan as she ate her pepperoni pizza slice.

"I sure am. It's been a nice break so far, ghosts and all." He smiled at her. "When I had to choose Thanksgiving with you or my uncle, the choice was easy. You're prettier."

She laughed, and the rest of the night passed easily. They had more pizza and then a few beers before they left. They were both in no hurry to get back to Magnolian, though neither of them said it.

Everyone was already in bed by the time they got home, and tomorrow, the day before Thanksgiving, promised to be a long day, so they said their good nights with a lingering kiss and went to bed.

Lillian dreaded turning off the lamp after she slipped in between the sheets, but she knew she needed the sleep. She gathered the little calico cat next to her in bed. Renae had shown up in the room just minutes after Lillian locked the door. The cat's favorite spot was apparently under her bed. Hopefully, the dream wouldn't come tonight, she thought. And it didn't. The night and next day passed with little fanfare and much preparation. Thanksgiving would not be so easy, though, she sensed with Will and Donovan both at the table.

Chapter 15

For as nightingales do upon glow-worms feed, So poets live upon the living light.
—Philip James Bailey

Thanksgiving morning passed quickly with Lillian and Donovan helping Leticia in the kitchen with all the dishes that had to be prepared. The day became more cheery with lots of laughter and flying flour, but Lillian was dreading Will's arrival with Monica on his arm. She tried to forget about it and was angry that she cared so much.

The food was on the sideboard and on the table set to go, and the family and servants were all seated. Grand's eyes were sparkling, and again, Lillian noticed how vital she looked. Aunt Lorelei was there, grumbling as usual and wearing a loud tent dress with two ugly turkeys on the front of it. Percy was grinning from ear to ear as he was likely to do on special occasions, and Leticia was moving like a blur from room to room with pots, pans, and serving trays.

Just as Leticia was pouring the drinks for everyone, the door opened in a gust of wind and a smattering of rain, and Will and Monica walked in. Will's eyes danced in their pale coolness, and he couldn't have looked more like a Norse God if he had tried. He was wearing cool tones of light blue and white, and his blond hair shone under the chandelier. Lillian's nervousness increased at the sight of him. Monica was no slouch at his side, either, with her long brown tresses flat ironed straight and gleaming and understated makeup. Her miniskirt showed off her tanned, stockinged legs to best advantage, as did the brown hue she was wearing. Lillian felt a hot dart of jealousy run through her. She forced herself to smile as big as she could. Monica returned the smile as greetings went all around.

She sensed Donovan looking at her and knew he hadn't missed her expression when Will had walked in the room. She plastered a smile on her face and squeezed his hand under the table.

Everything got quiet for a moment as Percy returned grace for the family and gave thanks for the year they had all had. His remembrance of "those who are no longer with us" and the specific naming of John Mullins brought Lillian to tears. She wiped them from the corner of her eyes, and Donovan squeezed her hand. The meal brought eating and bantering. Will and Donovan hit it off immediately which surprised Lillian. Will regaled Donovan with stories of destroying the prosecution in his law practice while Donovan described working with church ladies. Lillian felt her heart lighten. Perhaps the day would go well after all. At least everyone was behaving, and that was surprising enough. Even Aunt Lorelei joined in the laughter around the table.

After the first helping of turkey and all the sides, she got up to use the restroom. She padded down the hall behind the staircase. The restroom was all the way at the end, well away from the dining room. Before she could close the door, she heard Will's whisper.

"Don't close it. I just had to see you in private if only for a moment." Will smiled as he leaned against the door. Lillian closed the bathroom door and led him to the room next to it—the utility closet. The last thing she wanted to happen was to have someone stumble upon them in the hall. At least if she could get him in here, no one would see them standing there, chatting as if they had planned a hokey rendezvous near the bathroom. She sighed as she closed the utility room door.

Lillian stood in the middle of the room and looked at him in the dim light from the bulb.

"You were seeing me just fine across the table. After all, you have

Monica, and you two are chummy." Her voice was biting and louder than she had intended.

Will laughed under his breath. "You really don't get it, do you? I don't care about Monica. She's a nice person, a good looking girl, too, but she's not for me. I've never even kissed her, and believe me, she wanted me to." He leered at Lillian, and she rolled her eyes. "All of our dates have been a show—just for you. She doesn't know that, but that's why I've been running around town with her the last few days. I've known her for a while, but she's just a prop to keep your interest, Lillian." He put his hands on her waist, and she felt lightheaded.

"I don't believe you, and if she is, that's not a very nice thing to do to her." She swallowed hard.

"Nah, she's not the type to be easily heartbroken. Anyway, back to you and me. I just wanted to see you—alone. Since Donovan's been here, I've missed you." He backed her against the washing machine. Her pulse pounded in her neck.

"Will, I—this isn't a good time."

He interrupted her with his kiss, soft at first and then urgent, his body pressed against her. When he let her go, she was gasping, leaning on his chest. He stroked her hair.

"We'd better get back to the party, don't you think? You go first, and I'll follow. Be sure to fix your hair and your blouse. Your bra is showing." He winked at her.

She flushed and walked out of the room, his arms encircled her waist, and she could feel him behind her. He let her go outside the doorway. After taking a couple deep breaths, she thought she could handle acting normal again. It was obvious that their mutual absence had not been missed. Monica raised dark, sculpted brows at her, no smile on her face now. Lillian kept a blank face.

Donovan leaned over and whispered, "What was that all about?" She could hear the harsh anger in his tone.

She whispered in return, "I was using the restroom."

"Sure," he said with a frown. A few minutes later, Will came back to the table, a huge grin on his face. Lillian shot him daggers with her eyes.

Donovan was quiet through the rest of dinner. More plates were piled high, and then Percy turned on the football game afterward. Around nightfall, everyone started yawning. Some fixed third plates—Aunt Lorelei was on her fourth—and talked for a while. Grand went up to bed, and Will and Monica said their goodbyes.

"It was wonderful to meet you, Donovan. Good luck with the piano career." He shook the other man's hand sincerely, and admiration went through Lillian for a brief moment at how he had handled Donovan. Donovan, on the other hand, was quiet and muttered in return about the law practice.

Leticia, Donovan, and Lillian were left to clean up, and they did so, feeling exhausted by the end of the process. As they headed up to bed, Donovan stopped Lillian. She motioned him into her room, knowing he wanted to talk to her.

"We need to talk. I'm leaving tomorrow."

"What? Why?" She knew very well why, but she was still shocked. She felt ashamed that she had hurt Donovan so much.

"Well, it's been a nice trip, and I've enjoyed it, but my ticket is open, and tomorrow seems like a good time to go. There's a plane out of MGM that leaves every afternoon at twelve o'clock one-way to Pittsburgh." His mouth was set in a grim line.

"Donovan, I'm so sorry. I never meant to hurt you."

"Then you admit you're in love with him—that there's something going on between you two? Only a blind man wouldn't see it, and when you left and he followed you at lunch, I knew. I knew he had to see you, and that the Monica thing was all a charade. I can understand that. If I were in his shoes, I wouldn't want to be away from you for a second. You're too beautiful, Lillian." He held up his hand and put his finger to her lips, cutting off protests. "You haven't hurt me badly—yet, but I know how bad it feels to have a broken heart, and I'm trying to avoid that." He smiled faintly and then looked at her seriously. "One thing is that I'm still worried about you. If anything happens, you call me. I'll be here in a minute. Watch your step, and make sure the Viking looks after you." He smiled and enveloped her in a big hug.

Tears pricked her eyelids. "Thanks, Donovan. I might take you up on that. Hey, and I'll give you a call when I get back to Pittsburgh. Things are just crazy right now. This whole situation—"

"I know. It's okay. Take your space as long as you need it. You know where I'll be. For now, though, I'm taking myself out of the game as second choice. If I become first and only, let me know." He opened the door and went to his room. She heard his door shut softly.

Exhausted, Lillian trudged through the motions of her before-bed routine, feeling like she was going to fall over before she reached the bed. She turned the lamp off immediately and drifted into a sound sleep.

She was aware she was dreaming, but she was in her mother's role again—seeing through her eyes. Her mother was walking behind the house, heading toward the path to the water tower. The air was warm and muggy and lightning bugs danced among the trees—summer in the South. She fretted with each step she took. It was later than she had planned to go see him, but her mother kept coming up with things for her to do—almost as if she knew Gretchen had better plans for the evening, or part of it.

She was wearing red pedal pushers and a white, thin peasant blouse. She had daringly avoided wearing a bra, covering her chest up as she walked downstairs, hoping no one would see her. They hadn't. She lifted her chin, thinking that most young women avoided wearing bras these days when they could get away with it. She had taken care dressing this morning, knowing whom she was meeting later.

She entered the path, and the last rays of sun were going down ahead of her. She almost stopped in her path when she heard a lovely voice singing: Samson. He was singing a song she didn't know, but anything in that voice would have sounded like a bird of heaven. Gretchen kept walking, snapping limbs under her shoes, following the singing. There in the clearing by the water tower, away from prying eyes, he stood. His blue shirt gleaming in the fading light, and his jeans fit him like a second skin. Her breath caught in her throat. He was frowning.

"Well, why did you bring me here? You wanna play mistress of the manor? I got no time for that. I'm a grown man with a job to do, and I don't need to lose it fooling around with you." He put his hands by his side stiffly, as if to emphasize the point. She saw his eyes running over her.

"That's insulting and not why I brought you here." Gretchen smiled to soften her words. "I want to talk to you—to get to know you. I've been watching you, wanting to talk to you." She walked toward him, and he backed up a step.

"I don't think this is a good idea, Miss Gretchen."

"Call me Gretchen. We're equals."

He frowned. "So you say until you get angry with me or tired of me."

"What? I want to be your friend. Please take my intentions as the best." She was very close to him now after stepping closer and closer little by little. She saw him staring at her top. He moved his eyes away, turning red. She was pleased that she had gotten his attention.

"Okay, so what do you want to talk about, Gretchen?" And it started from there. They talked about books and music and all kinds of subjects as they sat on the ground, close together. The next thirty minutes of the dream were pure talk between them. It grew darker. The sky was periwinkle, changing to purple, when she laid a hand on his arm and hoisted herself up from the place they were sitting.

"See, I'm not so bad, am I?" She asked him, her violet eyes luminous in the fading light. She stood very close to him when he stood up.

He kissed her on the cheek, tentatively. "No, you're not." He took a shaky breath.

"I'll see you next Thursday then. I'll try to be earlier." She laid a warm hand on his arm and turned, walking back down the path. She burst out of the path, her heart as light as a feather. She went in the back door and murmured something to her mother, who was knitting a sweater for her. Then she skipped upstairs.

Lillian woke up at daybreak, the dream still fresh in her mind. She tossed and turned in the morning light as it dispelled the shadows of the night. Finally, she fell asleep again and didn't wake up until she heard a light tapping on her door.

"Want to walk me out? I have to go, or I'm not going to make my flight. I'll tell you one thing. I sure did sleep well last night." Donovan smiled.

"The sleep of the righteous, as they say." She smiled at him and followed him downstairs, still wearing her blue pajamas from the night before. She rubbed sleep out of her eyes and ignored the rumbling in her belly.

They walked outside into the pale sunlight of morning. The temperature was warmer today, and Lillian was happy to see the rain of yesterday banished.

"Well, this is it. Thanks for having me here. It was a nice break." Donovan smiled, but there was a hint of sadness in the droop of his eyes.

Lillian gave him a hard hug and stepped back. "You'll be hearing from me. Don't worry. I'll let you know the moment I get back in town, but I'll call you before that, too." She stepped away from him, giving him his distance if he wanted it.

"I want you to. I'm seriously nervous about leaving you here. I know that Percy and some other folks are looking out for you when you're under this roof, though." He sighed and turned, dangling his keys in hand and his carry-on behind him.

"I'll see you." He smiled and got into the car. Lillian stood beside it until he drove off. She waved him down the drive, her eyes misting over a little. She wondered if she was a fool for not begging him to stay—for letting him just walk away. No, she told herself firmly. You were only hurting him, and you don't know what you want right now.

Feeling depressed, she went back inside, determined to get ready and take a walk in the woods to clear her head. She felt driven, too, to go back to the water tower. All her dreams about Samson and her mother led there—over and over again. Her scalp prickled as she thought about it. After a quick shower, she headed downstairs, surprised to see Grand eating a late breakfast.

Lillian got a plate of fried ham, biscuits, and mixed fruit and sat down with her.

"So, Donovan left?" She looked at Lillian as she speared a piece of ham.

"Yes, just now." Lillian smiled, determined not to show that she was feeling a bit down as she slathered butter on a steaming biscuit.

"Ah, well. Then I guess it was just a quick trip, and he'll be back in Pittsburgh waiting for you when you decide to go. He certainly is a nice young man. You know, dear, you can always come back here any time. Don't feel that you must stay here and look after me. I would love you to, but I know you have your own life. I don't want you to jeopardize that for me. You don't find young men like Donovan just anywhere. Believe me, I know." Grand raised her eyebrows knowingly.

Lillian said, "I know, Grand. I need to stay here a bit longer. I've just been away for so long." She looked down at her plate and changed the subject. "I'm heading out for a walk," she said, just as Aunt Lorelei walked into the room. She told her good morning and then grabbed her light jacket from the coat rack and headed outside. The balmy air enlivened her, and she was glad she had decided to get away from it all. She needed some space to be alone and think. She rounded the corner of the house and headed to the woods, the breeze ruffling her hair like the breath of a lover.

Chapter 16

The sun glinted off of patches of damp grass, and the earth squelched under Lillian's boots with every step she took toward the water tower path. She was relieved to be outside where she could think. The air smelled of wet leaves and loamy earth. The scent was calming, and she breathed deeply. As she reached the head of the trail, she felt a dropping sensation in her stomach and almost turned back. She stopped herself from turning around and sprinting away. She had to face her fears and do what she could to help herself and those in Magnolian's past. Her own peace and safety and that of the house depended upon it. Everything grew still. She didn't hear any birds singing, where the moment before sparrows, blue jays, and all manner of feathered creatures had chirped in tandem after the rain. She clenched her fists against her own cowardice. She knew Samson was not to be feared. She just hated the feelings of despair she took on when he was near.

Taking a deep breath, she stepped on to the path and walked slowly, hearing the wet crunch of sticks and pine needles under her boots. Everything else was silent, as if the whole forest were waiting and she was the only person in it, or maybe the only person left on Earth. This must have been what Magnolian was like over a hundred years ago before this house had been built here. She could hear herself breathing in and out. She sped up her pace just a bit, her breath coming quickly, and in a few minutes, she could see the water tower. In front of it, she saw a shadowy figure. He was silent, but his arm was stretched out toward her. Her skin prickled, and goose bumps rose up on her arms. She was scared, and the air was growing colder.

Her breath puffed in and out, white even on a relatively warm autumn day.

She slowed her pace, hoping for and simultaneously dreading getting closer to him—her mother's first love. She could see the sheen of his brown skin as she got within yards of him. He was shiny, sparkling with dew like one of the surrounding trees after the rain. His face showed his devastation and longing, and she wanted to cry just looking at him and feeling his sadness. She couldn't seem to speak, so she just watched him and listened to the pregnant silence.

He made a circle around the water tower, walking slowly and gracefully. He made two more circles and then stopped. His eyes burned into hers—brown into violet. She knew that he wanted to tell her about the water tower. She was afraid to know what his message was. After the third circle around the tower, he stared at her until he vanished.

She stood there thinking little for a long time until she collapsed with shaky legs onto the damp grass. There she stayed for a while, and it came to her. Samson had been trying to tell her something important to him about that location, the tower area, and this wasn't the first time he had tried. He had met her here or nearby over and over again! She felt a frisson run through her. What if some evidence of what had happened to him was buried there? What if he himself was buried there? The thought of him being here and roaming in his current form for all these years made her feel such sorrow that she wanted to howl aloud. All she did was put her hands over her head and look at the ground, breathing deeply to steady herself. She felt a little better after a few minutes. Think rationally, she told herself. You can get through this if you think logically about what this might mean—that is, if ghosts were rational, she thought, and the thought brought a small smile to her face.

Feeling a bit better, she stood up and decided to walk slowly around the water tower just as Samson had done. The thought of it made her shiver, but she knew she had to do it. At least he was gone now, and the feeling of despair had lifted. She got half way around the first circle, the woods alive around her with the crackles of animal feet in the underbrush and the merry tweets of birds. She took a step and felt a peculiar sensation as if she were walking on someone's grave—a fear along with a certainty. I need Will, she thought instantly. He would come back here with her. He already had once, and he had offered any help he could give. She would just request that he tell no one and bring a shovel. That last bit made her smile in the midst of her fear. She felt a little more hopeful now, though still ready to get away from this spot.

She spent a few minutes scouring the grass and dirt patches near the tower for a landmark stick or something big enough to find on her return trip. She found a large stick and laid that on the place where she had felt a sense of having trespassed on a sacred spot. Then, she hurried back down the path to Magnolian, only half hearing the animals around her, brushing a cobweb out of her eyes as she made it halfway down the path. The sooner she could get back and talk to Will privately, the better. She had a sense of urgency, and her heart was racing as she burst out of the woods at a run. She decided to slow down to a regular walk, afraid that someone was watching her and might suspect something. It took all she could do to walk slowly and put a pleasant expression on over her tight features.

Lillian opened the front door of the house and plastered a smile on her face. No one was there to see it anyway, so she hurried upstairs, grabbing her cell phone and purse and locking the bedroom door behind her. She made a beeline down the steps, taking them two at a time and charging out the front door after grabbing the key to Grand's car.

As soon as she got in the car, she started it up and went, being careful not to peel out of the drive. She punched in Will's number and got no signal.

"No!" She yelled, shaking the phone in frustration. There was nothing for it but to keep driving out of the wooded area and on to the highway toward town. Will was most likely at home anyway since this was the Friday after Thanksgiving. That was if he hadn't decided to go to a nearby town and shop like so many others did on Black Fridays.

"Please God, let him be home," she prayed as she waited to turn left out on the main highway into town. Her phone rang just then, making her jump. The signal was back.

"Hello?" She said breathlessly.

"Lillian, it's me. Just wanted to tell you I'm back in Pittsburgh, safe and sound." Donovan sounded far away and forlorn.

"Thanks so much for letting me know. Was the trip good?" She hoped she sounded interested, but she was just distracted as she drove the two miles to town.

"It was. A nice and easy flight—always a good thing." He paused. "I miss you already. I hope you come home really soon. Let me know what your plans are. When you know, I mean." His voice was so soft, she could hardly hear him. With a pang, she remembered noticing that about him early on and liking it. Now, she thought it was more annoying than anything. Funny how swiftly feelings changed about someone, she thought, especially when someone else came into the picture.

"I will. I'll talk to you soon, Donovan. Don't let those church ladies get you down next week. Take care."

"You, too," he whispered.

She disconnected in mid-too, sighing as she quickly punched Will's number in again. It was busy now. He was probably canoodling with Monica in front of a roaring fire right now. The thought annoyed her. She cursed under her breath and kept driving toward his law office. The town was all but dead with everyone gone for Thanksgiving holidays. As expected, his Mercedes wasn't at the office. She turned down a side street to go to his house, praying he was there and hoping he wouldn't think she had flipped her lid finally with her strange request.

His car was there, and so was another sporty white number. Her stomach dropped. It could be anyone, she thought. It probably wasn't Monica. She inched by slowly since no one was behind her. Just then, Monica walked out of the front door, laughing. She turned and kissed Will on the cheek, putting her arms around him and pressing into him with a smile. Breathless and nearly blinded by tears, she sped on, going about a mile before she pulled the car over in an abandoned building lot and cried long and hard for a couple minutes. The only saving grace was that she was certain neither of them had seen her when she drove by.

When she finally had control of herself, she wiped her tears and thought about her options. She didn't see that she had many. How could she turn to Will now when everything he had said to her had been a lie? Defeated, she drove back toward Magnolian slowly. When she passed Will's door, both cars were gone. So, that's it, she thought. They're together. The thought made her chest hurt in a way she had never experienced. She thought she understood the term "heartache" now.

As she turned in to Magnolian, a fog of depression descended over her. She didn't know what to do. She wanted to head back to Pittsburgh—hop a plane tomorrow and get out of here, leave the ghosts and the mess behind. She knew she couldn't do that, though. Samson's eyes would haunt her, as would her mother's journal. There would be no escape from what she knew.

She parked and dragged herself out of the car, trudging up the steps and into the house. She had come in just in time for dinner. In her despair, she hadn't noticed Will's Mercedes parked to the far left corner of the drive.

"Hi, gorgeous." He smiled at her and stabbed a piece of chicken.

Chapter 17

"What are you doing here?" Her question came out in a childish squeak. She sat down with a flop at the dining room table. All eyes were on her. She decided not to ask anything else.

"Eating dinner. I was invited to leftovers." Will grinned around a mouthful of dressing. "Thanks again for calling to invite me, Aunt Lorelei."

Aunt Lorelei, of all people! What was this world coming to? Then Lillian noticed Aunt Lorelei's simpering smile and realized that she liked any Tate she could get to come over and give her the time of day—Joe or Will would do just fine. She stifled an exhausted giggle, got up, and served herself a heaping plate from the sideboard along with a cold glass of sweet tea. She figured she might as well eat up. She hadn't realized how hungry she was until she saw dinner. She had been totally immersed in Samson's agony and her own over Will. She would grin and bear dinner and then get him alone as soon as she could to talk about plans.

No one was in a particularly talkative mood, and she was glad of it. Grand had stayed upstairs and had a tray taken to her. Percy and Leticia were joining them for a rare evening at the table. Lillian was sure it had been at Will's insistence. Having Aunt Lorelei all to himself might not have been as great as it sounded. She almost choked on a piece of turkey, trying not to laugh at her thoughts.

"So, Donovan's gone, I take it?" Will looked at her wide eyed, as if this were news to him.

"Yes, he's back in Pittsburgh." She wanted him to know that they had been in contact.

"Oh, great. I hope he liked our little bit of the country. It wasn't the best time to see it, but at least everything isn't covered in snow." He wiped his mouth with a napkin, his blue eyes dancing with suppressed laughter.

"He did. He just had things he had to attend to." She looked at him with a hard stare, remembering Monica pressed against him, her long legs shown to advantage in a blue miniskirt. It seemed that was the only type of clothing the woman had, she thought with a frown.

"I understand. Well, I'm glad he came down. He is a good friend, isn't he?" Will's sardonic tone was not missed by Lillian or anyone else at the table. Everyone was looking down at their food but Lillian and Will.

"The best," she said, intending to wound. "He came to my father's funeral. I had no idea he was going to show up. He was there for me at a time when virtually no one else was." Lillian stared at Will, her mouth trembling. She might not be in love with Donovan, but he was a true friend, and Will would not take that away from him.

"I'm so glad to hear it," Will said with a tiny smile. She was happy to see that the dagger had hit home. He drank his last sip of coffee and flashed a smile around the table.

"Thanks again for the invite this evening. The food was even more delicious the second time around, but I have to be going. I have a killer brief to finish this weekend." He stood up and stretched his back, showing off his tight torso under his t-shirt. Damn him, thought Lillian. If it was possible, the man was even more beautiful in a t-shirt and jeans than he was in power suits.

She got up without a word and followed him out the door. On the porch, he stopped and turned around with a big smile.

"Something you need to say?" He folded his arms and leaned on the porch post, so sure of himself she wanted to smack him.

"Yes, there is, but I don't want to say it here. Can we go somewhere for coffee—somewhere nice and quiet without a lot of nosy people or crowds? My treat," she added with a sickly sweet grin she didn't feel.

"Crowds in Everwood? Nah. I know just the place. I'll drive." She followed him to his car, watching him walk and hating herself for it.

They pulled out of the driveway in silence. Once they were turning on to the highway, he spoke. "I'm sorry Donovan left. I wasn't trying to run him off. Did he leave because of me?" His tone was innocent.

"No." She wanted to perturb him. Let him figure it out for himself!

"Good, I'm glad to hear that." He moved his right hand over to her knee and kept it there. She could feel the heat of his palm through her jeans. She liked the way it felt there, but she wasn't going to play his game anymore.

"Get your hand off of me." She snapped at him.

"What? What's wrong with you?" He sounded truly mystified, which only made her angrier.

"You know what! You telling me you love me and need me and then sleeping with Monica—like I'm an idiot!" Her breath was coming fast.

"What are you talking about? Did you see Monica's car at my house this afternoon?" He smiled at her, relishing her anger.

"Yes, and I saw her kissing on your face, too." She knew she sounded juvenile, but she couldn't help it. "Her and her miniskirts. Is that all the woman owns to wear?"

"Maybe," he grinned. "She knows how to play to her strengths, I guess. But Lily, seriously, she had just come by to get a brief. She always kisses me on the cheek when she leaves. Like I said, she wants more than friendship, but I'm not into that with her. She's a nice girl, but she's not my type." He looked at her, his expression serious now.

"I just don't know if I believe you." Lillian's heart had slowed, and she looked at him.

"I'm sorry to hear that. You can. I promise you."

She cleared her throat, not wanting to talk about it further. "I didn't ask you to go somewhere with me because of that anyway. I need something from you." Her voice was full of steel.

"And I'm here now, so what do you need?" He put his hand back on her leg, running it up near the top of her thigh. She shivered and didn't ask him to stop. He took his hand away and put it back on the wheel, smiling at her.

"You're going to think it's crazy, but hear me out." She looked at him, intent on convincing him to go along with her.

"I went back to the water tower yesterday and saw Samson. He walked around the water tower several times—as if he were trying to tell me something about that spot. He has been in there before—as you know or at least as I've told you when we were together, and Donovan felt him there, too."

Will interrupted her. "He did? Donovan felt him just like you do?"

"Yes, he did. It made me feel relieved. I mean, I knew he was there and that I'd seen and felt him at the water tower, but no one else had."

"Good. I'm glad he felt the things you did, then." Will looked sincere as he said it.

She stopped and cleared her throat. "Anyway, perhaps he's still there—Samson, I mean—and I don't mean just in spirit." She looked at Will intently.

He gazed back at her as they pulled into Ida's Coffee Shop—a local place with warm booths and a chic ambiance. They walked in silently and took a seat in a brown leather booth. A young waitress with thick eyeliner took their order, smiling at Will the whole time. After she left, he leaned closer to Lillian across the table.

"I believe you, and I think you might be right. I mean, we have no evidence that anyone else at Magnolian has even seen Samson—I mean as he currently manifests. I know Donovan has sensed him, but he doesn't live there. He was just visiting." He wrinkled his brow in thought. "So the question is, what should we do about it?"

"I have an idea. I want you to go out there with me. I got a feeling about one particular spot that I walked over and stood on, and I've marked it with a thick branch for now. I want to take a couple shovels and start digging." She squeezed his hand across the table.

Will whistled softly. "That's quite a plan you have there, ma'am. Ok, I'm game—but not tonight. How about tomorrow night under cover of darkness? I could meet you on the path and not even come by the house. We don't need to clue in whoever it is that had something to do with this—if it's murder we're talking about here. And if we find anything, we have to take it straight to the police. That's the deal. Otherwise, I don't help. What do you say, Lily?"

He grew silent as the waitress brought their coffees.

"Thanks." He gave her a megawatt smile which she returned, not even glancing at Lillian.

"Must you always do that?" Lillian grimaced at him.

"What?" His eyes were big and innocent.

"Never mind. It's not important right now." She sighed. "I think your plan will work. So, tomorrow is act natural Saturday for me, and we'll meet at the water tower tomorrow night. What time?"

"When does everybody turn in at Magnolian? Early, right?" He sipped his hot coffee and stirred in a packet of raw sugar.

"Yeah, usually around ten." Lillian drank a sip of her latte.

"All right, then we give them some time to get to sleep, and you sneak out. I'll expect you there by eleven thirty. I might get there a few minutes early and start digging if I can find your big limb by the tower. If we find something, we need to take it to the police as I said. They can handle it from there."

"I agree, but this is between you and me for now. Don't tell anyone—not even your dad." She looked at him over her coffee cup.

"Why would I tell him? What are you getting at?" Light dawned in his eyes, and he looked angry. "Do you think he had something to do with Samson's disappearance? Are you nuts?" His voice got louder and she shushed him with a finger to her lips.

"No, well, I don't know. It wouldn't look good for him if a Stark were dating a black man, would it? What a scandal then and now. He was running for mayor, and now he's up for governor." She slid her eyes away, feeling bad about suggesting it.

"I get your point, but I don't appreciate your accusation or train of thought, but alright. Let's just leave that for now. The important thing is to see if there is even anything there for us to worry about, okay?" He looked at her, his eyes still hard chips of blue.

"I agree." She sighed quietly in relief.

They finished their coffees in relative silence, both deep in thought. Lillian didn't miss the worried frown that had settled on Will's face. Did he, too, suspect his father of having a role in Samson's fate? She reached out impulsively and squeezed his hand.

"I'm sorry for what I said. No more jumping to conclusions. I promise."

He lifted her hand and kissed her fingers, making her feel warm all over. "It's okay. This is your mother's life and her first love's— Percy's grandson—you are talking about here. It's important, and we should keep open minds. Ready to go?" They drove back to Magnolian in subdued silence. Lillian had a funny feeling in the pit of her stomach, and she sensed Will was nervous, too.

They pulled into the drive way, and Will pecked her on the cheek. "Act cool. Meet me tomorrow evening—no later than 11:30. If you can find a shovel or some tools in the shed secretly without a bunch of fuss, do that, and if you need to call me about anything before then, do it away from the house—if you can. And be careful." He gave her a long look, and she read his feelings for her and his worry in it.

She nodded. "Thanks so much. I appreciate this more than you'll ever know." With a quick smile, she hopped out of the car, noticing how dark the house looked tonight, as if it were watching them and listening—or more likely as if one of its supposed sleepers were awake in the darkness, looking out. That thought made her shiver. She grimaced at her nervous thoughts and went inside, the front porch steps creaking like moaning old women in the dim light. The house was full of shadows, except for the sitting room lamp that illuminated only a corner of that room. Walking carefully, she climbed the stairs silently, looking at her mother's portrait as she passed. Tonight, she fancied that Gretchen was looking back at her, waiting, too, to see if her daughter would find out what had happened on that night so many years ago. She had a strange feeling her mother was hoping in her, but that must be fanciful imagination. She touched the portrait silently, feeling a strong bond with her mother. She climbed the rest of the stairs to her room.

When she unlocked her bedroom, she undressed and got ready for bed quickly. She was tired, but her mind was racing, and her heart bumped unsteadily in her chest. To calm her nerves, she took a copy of Frances Burney's novel *Evelina* off of the shelf. She had always loved the shy heroine, but tonight, she was counting on it to put her to sleep quickly. She read until her eyes finally grew heavy and her mind was distracted before she flipped off the lamp. She slept like the dead until morning and was grateful for it.

Chapter 18

*Hark! ah, the nightingale—The tawny-throated! Hark from that
moonlit cedar what a burst! What triumph! hark!—what pain!....
Again—thou hearest? Eternal passion! Eternal pain!*
—from "Philomela" by Matthew Arnold

The day dawned bitterly cold as was obvious by how frozen
Lillian's ears were as she slowly opened her eyes. The room felt icy,
though she could see that the curtains were billowing in the heat
flowing from the heater vents near them. It was definitely her coldest
day yet in the sunny South. At least the sun was shining out of a hard,
white sky.

"Brrr." She said under her breath, moving stiffly out of bed. Then,
she remembered what she was going to do today and groaned,
wishing for a warmer day. She took a quick shower, trembling in the
cold air and hearing the wind moaning like a spirit in unrest outside
the window. That thought made her think of Samson, and she put him
out of her mind, not wanting to dwell on the happenings of the past
weeks—at least not now. Tonight would offer plenty of time for
thinking about what had been happening for the past few weeks and
what had happened almost forty years ago—she hoped. She was
nervous that something would happen before tonight to stop her plans.
She smiled at herself in the mirror, thinking it was best not to borrow
trouble.

Dressing in two layers on top, she buttoned her jeans and put
some lip gloss on quickly. As she headed down to breakfast, she
heard the sound of the television blaring from the living room.

Detouring that way, she went in to find Aunt Lorelei sitting in the middle of the couch, eyes glued to the flat screen television where the newscaster was predicting temperatures in the lower thirties and snow by nightfall.

"Bad weather coming," Aunt Lorelei said, eying her with seeming pleasure in this turn of events.

"Yeah, it looks like it." Lillian suppressed a frustrated sigh as she leaned against the back of the couch. It wouldn't be the best digging weather, that was for sure.

"Hope you didn't have any big plans. Most things close around here when it snows. Hardly ever does, you know—well, not until January if it's going to. The roads get slippery, and people wreck like crazy. They don't know how to drive in the snow like you Yankees do." She said this last bit sharply but with a little smile, shifting her purple clad bulk on the couch.

"I'm sure it's tough when that happens," Lillian said, distracted.

Aunt Lorelei didn't say anything else, and Lillian walked out and went to the dining room to get some breakfast before going out to Percy's shed to see what she could find in the way of supplies for the evening's adventure. She wanted to gather up the tools and put them behind the house to take with her later tonight. No one would be going out there anyhow today. She ate her eggs and bacon in silence, no one accompanying her at the table but the shrieking wind outside.

She remembered to go back upstairs and rummage for a bag to put small tools in—flashlights and batteries, for example, for this evening. She shoved the bag under her thick sweater on her way out of her bedroom and locked the door as always. As she walked downstairs, she still heard the weather forecaster droning on in a Southern accent about the impending possible snow and certain cold temperatures. She sighed and braced herself for the unwelcome chill when she went outside.

She shoved the bag in her pocket and her hands in her pockets, too, as she headed for the shed over to the far right of the house. She had already swung the rusty, creaky door open when she realized someone was inside. Timmy.

He looked at her with a question but didn't say anything as he swept the floor around Percy's work bench. She knew that was the place where he fashioned critters out of spare metal parts and wood like pigs, donkeys, frogs, and more.

Lillian walked with measured steps through the door, hoping to get a chance to talk to the small, slope-shouldered boy.

"I'm—I'm just looking for some tools. I'm planning a late night walk, and I found an old artifact in the woods I want to explore further." She smiled, trying to look normal as her heart pounded.

"Arrowheads? We have a lot of those around in various places." The boy's voice was curiously high pitched and monotone. "Percy don't care. Take what you want. Just be sure to bring it back. I don't want to get into trouble." He smiled nervously and was about to shuffle past her, heading out the door. She was relieved that he didn't seem to care what she was going to do with the tools.

"I'll bring them back very soon. I promise. Wait, Timmy. Can I talk to you?" His big brown eyes shifted under his heavy brows and he looked away from her, fiddling with rope he had in his hand. "I guess, but I have to go soon and find Percy. He's got work for me to do." He moved from one foot to the other.

"Okay. That's fine. I'm just wondering if you've seen anything strange around here lately. You know I've had some accidents. I don't know if you've heard," she said softly, willing the boy to make eye contact. He made for the door instead, his back turned toward her.

"No," he mumbled. "Don't know anything about that." He was breathing so hard, she could see it through his shabby brown coat.

"All right, then," she said gently. "I appreciate you taking the time to talk to me. If you think of anything or see anything that seems strange, please find me and let me know. And thanks for all the hard work you do around Magnolian." She smiled at him, and he half looked at her.

He rushed past her and out the door like a man being chased by demons as he said, "Okay, I will, Miss Lillian." His words were distorted by a speech impediment, and Lillian felt pity for him. What a hard life he must have had to this point! She liked Percy all the more for taking him under his wing here at Magnolian and giving him a place to thrive as he saw fit. She promised herself to check up and make sure he had everything he needed here and wherever he lived.

Lillian breathed out heavily and wondered if he would tell anyone he had seen her there, and if he did, would they have any idea what she was up to? Feeling spooked, she looked over the shiny tools quickly and grabbed a sturdy but small shovel, three flashlights, and rechargeable batteries clearly labeled in black permanent marker in small and large bins. Thank God for Percy's organization. As she put the flashlights and batteries in her bag, she heard a skittering sound and shivered at the unseen rats or roaches. She wasn't sticking around to find out. The cold weather always brought them inside any warmer place than the outdoors in the South. She shoved the door open and pulled the string to turn the light off, hurrying out the door, shutting it and bolting it behind her. Scampering across the lawn, she rounded the side of the house and put the tools in the ruined garden in a thick bush that still flourished. She didn't think anyone would come out here, let alone mess with them before late tonight when she came back to get them.

Blowing on her hands to warm them up, she headed back for the house, feeling nervous about waiting it out. It was only mid-morning, but she figured she could read or surf the net to pass some time. The main thing was not to get into a tizzy about her plans for the evening and rouse suspicion, she thought. Taking a deep breath, she opened the front door. Grand was in the sitting room, reading by a crackling fire.

"Come, dear. Sit down for a bit," she gestured to the couch near her.

"I think I will. The fire is so cozy," she said, warming hands together.

The flames leaped up and reflected off of Grand's face. "Yes, I always like a fire in the cold, don't you?"

"I do, Grand. We lit the fire quite often in Pennsylvania." She stopped herself, noticing how automatically she had used the past tense in that sentence—as if her life there were in the past. "How are you feeling today?" She settled back on the couch, enjoying the time with her grandmother.

"Pretty good today, dear. I figured I could at least sit down here and read a while or chat with you if you came down." Grand looked into the fire.

Lillian felt a pang. She hadn't been ignoring Grand, but she had been so busy the last few days that she hadn't spent much time with her. She vowed to herself to change that, starting now.

"How about a game of checkers, Grand? It's been a while. Think you can still beat me like you used to?" She smiled, hoping she had struck on something to take her mind off of her errand for the night.

"I do. I'm even better than I was then, dear. I'd love to play!" Grand's eyes lit up with delight. "They're just in the chest over there if you would get them out."

Lillian went over to the chest sitting across the room by the peach love seat and grabbed the old checkers game. They spent a lively afternoon playing and drinking the hot Lady Grey tea Leticia offered them mid-game. Grand won the majority of the games, just as she had predicted she would be able to do. Then, protesting that she was worn out, she headed upstairs for lunch in her room and a nap. "I might need my rest for later. I don't like to be tired out when snow is predicted. I like to try to stay up and see the first flakes from my window. We get so little snow after all. It takes me right back to my childhood. We used to get more here—usually in January or February. I remember building snowmen outside on the front lawn of Magnolian with my sister, Mary Lou. She died as a child, you know," she said with a sad smile.

"I'm so sorry, Grand. I remember dad mentioning her once, I think. I'm glad you have happy memories with her and that snow reminds you of those times. I guess I'm sick of snow, seeing it as often as I do in Pittsburgh, but I obviously take it for granted." She would have to be extra quiet and sneaky tonight if Grand was going to stay up later than usual. Hopefully, it was all talk, and she would be out like a light at nine o'clock.

Grand's laugh tinkled like a tiny silver bell as she headed up the stairs. "I can imagine you are, dear. Stay inside and warm up. Have some hot cocoa with your lunch if you'd like, too."

"I just might, Grand," Lillian said, getting up and heading toward the kitchen for lunch. She sniffed the air on her way, and the smell of fresh potato soup made her stomach rumble. Her appetite was back in full force today. Ladling out a big bowl from the sideboard and getting some hot, just-buttered wheat rolls to go with it as well as a small salad, she sat down at the table, wolfing it all down. She wondered, not for the first time, what it was about cold weather that always affected her appetite. Feeling warm and a bit drowsy, she decided to take a nap this afternoon, too. After all, it would be a long night.

She spent the afternoon huddled under her comforter and an extra quilt she found in the small bedroom closet. Thinking of her mother sleeping under that same quilt many years ago gave her a feeling of comfort. How many cold days or evenings had she spent under this quilt, dreaming of Samson, happy and later, heartbroken? She slept deeply, and when she woke up, it was nearly dinner time. Not being able to face the rest of the family, she decided to go out for a bite on her own. That would help pass some of the hours between now and late night.

No one was downstairs when she got there, so she scrawled a quick note, letting Grand know that she was going out for a bite to eat, adding that she didn't want to get stir crazy before the snow got here. It sounded like a good excuse, she thought, putting the pen on the table and pulling on her gray coat as she headed out to Grand's car.

As she wheeled down the drive, she noticed the stark white of the sky against the dark branches. That sky definitely spelled snow at any time, she thought. She would have to make dinner quicker than she would have liked. She drove through town, noticing the streets were even lonelier than usual. Everyone must have already gathered supplies for the snow and gotten indoors. She turned in to the Waffle House, thinking warm pancakes and coffee sounded like just the thing. A few others already sat in the booths there, but she had one side of the restaurant all to herself. She sat, lost in thought, until a waitress came to take her order.

"What'll you have, hon?" The waitress's skin was leathery, like she had baked in the sun for years without a break. She couldn't have been much over forty, so her preserved look was even more shocking.

"The pancake special and coffee please." Pancakes seemed perfect on a cold evening.

"All righty. It'll be right out, hon. You know they're calling for snow this evening, doncha? Better get home before too late. It's gonna get crazy out there with snow on the roads." The waitress looked at her, penciled on brows raised in a question.

"Yes, I've heard about it. I just wanted to get out one more time before that happened." Lillian smiled as the waitress strode briskly away. People in Everwood definitely tried to look out for you if they could. She liked that and wondered again about going back to Pittsburgh. Oh, the people there were friendly enough, but something about the big city combined with the cold and gray of several months a year took the edge off of any warmth they had. It got used up faster just dealing with the concerns of everyday life.

Lillian was more nervous than she had ever been—or remembered being, anyway, she thought with a grimace. Breathing deeply, she told herself that Will would be with her. How wrong could things go? Hopefully by the early morning, they would have some answers to the questions plaguing her, and Samson would soon be at rest, the past righted.

Her food came quickly, and she enjoyed every sticky bite of the thick pancakes, dripping with extra butter and warm syrup. The eggs that came with them weren't bad either. Fortified for the night ahead, she paid her bill and walked out into the cold. The snow hadn't started yet, and it was almost nine o'clock. She hoped it would not start at all.

The drive back to Magnolian was quiet. Her heart was pounding already, and she had over an hour to wait before she could meet Will—if he showed up in this cold. She knew he would and that the thought was silly. She knew enough to trust him to be there. She pulled into the driveway at Magnolian, and all the lights were out but one—Grand's. Lillian could even see her shadow in the window as she looked out, looking for snow, Lillian assumed. That brought a grin to her face, in spite of herself. She walked up the front door and went inside quietly. The house was quiet. Only the ticking of the clock sounded in her ears. She swallowed hard as she headed upstairs.

Chapter 19

To the red rising moon, and loud and deep the nightingale is singing from the steep.
—Henry Wadsworth Longfellow

She quietly changed into warm socks, boots, a stocking cap she had luckily thrown in her suitcase at the last minute, and warmer corduroy pants, and kept her long-sleeved shirt and sweater on. She paced a little and then got mad at herself and sat on the bed to read. Before she knew it, it was eleven o'clock—time to sneak out and get her bag from its hiding place. She had only heard the creaks of the house and was sure everyone was asleep.

She turned her doorknob quietly, locking it behind her with a muffled click of the key in lock. She glided on the wooden floor of the landing and quietly down the carpeted steps. She touched her mother's picture gently on the edge as she went down. She listened as she descended, but heard nothing. She went through the sitting room and living room and to the back door, unlocking it silently as she exited. She knew where the spare key was—under the flower pot, at least it always had been. She checked quickly. It was still there. She didn't want to get locked out for the night or have to pound on a door to be let in. That would lead to some explaining for sure, she thought.

She made her way stealthily in the cold quiet to the thick bush where her supplies were hidden. Her hands were cold, and she quickly slipped on the thick work gloves she had found in the shed. Grabbing the small shovel and the bag, she made her way toward the path, flashlight in her right hand, leading the way, throwing yellow beams on frosty ground. Every cracking limb or movement of an animal made her heart skip a beat. She was frightened, though she wasn't sure why exactly. It was just darkness, but then darkness had been an old enemy of man and woman. An enemy that had driven them to learn to start fires to stay warm and cast light on the things that prowled in the dark. Laughing softly at her imaginings, she continued to the water tower path, her feet crunching pine needles and cones. She hurried down the path, her breath coming in sharp puffs due to her fear and her wish to see Will soon.

The flashlight beam arced crazily through the trees, and she saw a pair of red eyes peeping at her from behind a bush. It's just a cat or a bunny, she told herself even as her mind pointed out other more frightening possibilities. Weeds and branches clawed at her legs as if trying to stop her progress down the path, and she cried out softly when a sharp jagged bush penetrated through her jeans. When she burst into the clearing, she could have sobbed, so great was her relief to be out of the wooded path. The water tower stood in spooky white relief against the sky in which no stars shone. It was its only light, and it was looming like a monster that had defeated its hopeless prey.

Swallowing hard, Lillian sat down, holding the flashlight in shaking hands after putting the shovel and bag down. Will wasn't there yet, and Lillian shivered in the chill of the night. She thought of happy times in her life—of parties and boys and other things that brought a smile to her face. She needed to divert her thoughts from the night and the threats in it—both living and dead. Sitting in the clearing, she had her back to the water tower path and facing the one Will would come up from the road with his car. She sat still for a few minutes, and her mind went elsewhere. She was not sure if she was awake or sleeping when Samson appeared before her as he had that night so long ago after being hounded through the woods with Gretchen.

She traveled along with him somehow—as if she were floating above him as her father had done in her dreams. He had turned down the path to his house after kissing Gretchen goodbye for the night. He had just left the water tower path when a shadow loomed in front of him. The figure was masked, and an arm was raised. He felt an explosion in his skull, and everything went dark.

Lillian was sobbing, fully awake now. So, that's how Samson had died—with a crack to the skull. It had been hard enough to kill him, she was sure. Shivering, she longed for Will to come along. She looked at the glowing hands of her watch. It was 11:17 by the green lit hands. She wasn't sure if she had ever felt so alone, and she considered leaving the woods, but she knew she had to see this thing through for all of their sakes. Lillian was so lost in thought that she didn't hear the light footfall behind her or feel the butt of the gun against her head until it was too late and darkness over took her sight.

She awoke fuzzy-headed to voices: Will's and another that she had to take a moment to place. Grand's voice, but a twisted, angry version of it. Lillian realized she was tied with her hands behind her back to a tree on the side of the clearing next to the water tower path entrance. She moaned as her head throbbed. What was Grand doing here? Why wouldn't Grand untie her, Lillian wondered, not being able to make sense of things. As she focused fully on her surroundings, she realized Will was pleading with Grand.

"Mrs. Stark—Beverly. It's okay. I'll leave and never come back. I won't tell anyone about anything." He had his hands out in front of him as if to show he meant no harm. His eyes were the widest Lillian had ever seen them.

Her grandmother cackled in a harsh voice that made Lillian shiver. Grand was standing in front of her, a few yards away, facing Will. She was wearing slippers, leggings, and a tight fitting shirt, the likes of which Lillian had never seen her wear. She had a handgun pointed at Will, and it looked like she knew how to use it.

"You don't know anything to tell. You're trespassing on my land, and this is the last time you will." Grand stood erect and strong, to Lillian's disbelief. How in the world could she look so healthy? A creeping thought came to her, and she shivered. Had the whole sickness been an act—from the staying in bed to the fainting and everything else? But why? Tears filled her eyes.

"I got rid of that nigger Samson Jones, and I can get rid of you, too. You won't threaten my family like he did. Troublemakers get what's coming to them, no matter who they are." Grand snarled at him, showing teeth like a rabid dog moving in for the kill.

Lillian croaked some sounds without words and then found her voice. "But why are you doing this, Grand? I don't understand." She knew now that Grand had hit Samson over the head and killed him all those years ago. She supposed she had also dragged his body down the path and buried him. Her teeth chattered. She couldn't stop them, and her wrists ached from being tied with rope.

"Why? What do you mean, girl? Why?" Grand laughed as if something were very funny. "Your mama thought she was so smart—so progressive. That she was different and could do what she wanted with no mind to convention and how things were done before. Well, she wasn't. She was a little fool just like any other white girl who went for a young buck like Samson. I wasn't going to stand by and let her ruin the family name with her black husband or her half breed children. So, I killed him." She turned to Lillian and grinned, the light of her flashlight shining up on her face, distorting it like a hideous mask.

Lillian groaned. "Grand, they loved each other. They really did," she whispered. "It would have been okay." Now nothing is okay, she thought to herself with despair.

"Mrs. Stark, just let Lillian go. She can leave—go back to Pittsburgh on the first flight tomorrow. I'll never touch her or talk to her again. Just let her go."

"I will, don't you worry, after I take care of you." She cocked the gun, and Lillian moaned.

"Grand, please don't. I'll do anything you ask. Spare Will."

"I won't, and you're leaving tomorrow, just as he said. If you say a word about any of this—you have no proof anyway, and there will be no body to find—I'll ruin your life. You will never inherit Magnolian." Grand's voice rose in triumph with these last words as Lillian stared at her dumbfounded. Grand really thought she would sacrifice the love of her life for Magnolian. At the same moment, Lillian realized that she had admitted to herself that Will was the love of her life.

She looked at him, searing his image in her mind forever—his blond curls gleaming in the light of Grand's flashlight and his face set in determination. Lillian felt as if her heart was squeezed in a giant's merciless hand at the thought of never laughing with him again or putting up with his flirting.

Grand half turned to her to say something, distracted by the taste of her coming victory over all who would challenge the Starks and Magnolian, and Will took that moment to rush at her. He wrenched the gun from her hand and pushed her to the ground. She screamed and scrambled on the ground, trying to regain her footing. He took the butt of the gun and hit her on the head—hard enough to knock her out.

Lillian screamed, "Grand!" Will ran to Lillian and gathered her in his arms. She was too shocked to cry. He untied her quickly and pulled his cell phone out. "I have reception. Thank God," he breathed, his breath coming fast as white spirals in the air. He punched in numbers rapidly—his father's and then 911. She half heard what he said in the calls. Her mind was buzzing.

As he was hanging up on the second call, Lillian was distracted by an image behind him—Samson had materialized just feet from them, and he was smiling with such love and gratitude at her that she sobbed anew. His face gave off sparks of light, and it seemed that he floated between two planes of existence. He was clearly fading from this one, though, and his presence was less than she had ever felt it. She would find his body and lay him to rest, but the menace to Magnolian was no more.

"Will, look!" She pointed behind him, but Samson was gone and he saw nothing. He turned back to her, puzzled as he helped her off the ground and held on to her. She hugged him tightly, feeling the fuzzy material of his green pullover on her cheek, and then let go so he could keep watch over Grand. Tears flowed down her cheeks silently, feeling cold in the icy air. The first snowflake hit her nose as she stood there, waiting. More followed, pattering quietly to the ground and disappearing forever.

Grand moaned, and Will trained the gun on her. Lillian was relieved to hear her grandmother make a noise. In minutes, sirens screamed nearby, and two police cars roared into the clearing. Joe Tate's truck soon followed, and he jumped out and ran to them. It was over, Lillian thought with sadness and relief mingled, or had it only begun?

Chapter 20

O nightingale, that on yon bloomy spray Warblest at eve, when all the woods are still; Thou with fresh hope the lover's heart dost fill While the jolly hours lead on propitious May.
—from "Sonnet—to the Nightingale" by John Milton

That night was a long one—passing in a blur of cold and shock. Lillian and Will went to the hospital to be with Grand. Will drove them both in his car, right behind the ambulance. After she was stabilized, Lillian was allowed to go in and see her for a few minutes. She walked into the room slowly, heart thudding painfully in her chest to see the woman she had thought she had known, lying in the bed, looking so diminished and angry—still angry. The green hospital walls and fake plastic fern in the corner only added to the surreal nature of the room. Grand no more fit there than she would have in a regular house. Lillian could see how coupled she was with Magnolian once she was removed from the familiar setting. She realized that she was unafraid for the first time in weeks. This woman posed no threat to anyone now. Her kingdom had always been a small one, and that night had dethroned her for good.

"Lillian, I want to tell you something." Grand's voice was a scratchy whisper. She clutched at the thin white bed sheet, looking like a strange child playing dress up with the hospital gown on. How many times had Lillian seen her in bed in her best dressing gown? It must feel like a comedown to be like all the other mortals in their skimpy cotton gowns.

"Yes, Grand?" Lillian's voice was cold, and she didn't move

closer to her grandmother. She sat in the green vinyl chair some feet away from the bed. She just couldn't bring herself closer to the woman after knowing the damage she had inflicted on her own daughter and the man that daughter had loved. Still, tears threatened behind her eyes. This woman was not the same one who had put Band-Aids on skinned knees or laughed with her over Donovan and Will, surely not?

"Don't cry. I'm sorry you're upset. I just did what I had to do for your mama and for Magnolian. That house was the only thing that mattered to me. Well, the house and what it meant about who I was. I was a Stark—a leader in Everwood. I was expected to hold to certain standards, and I did, no matter the cost." She looked stonily at Lillian, her eyes blazing like flowers in brilliant sunlight.

Lillian bit back a retort and folded her trembling hands in her lap, knowing Grand wouldn't understand or care what she thought. Her grandmother stared into the distance as she went on, talking in the direction of the wall or the mounted, silent television.

"Before you came to Magnolian, he haunted me almost every night—in my room. At first, it was cold. Then, I saw him, and I knew him right away. He was so angry. His eyes blazed at me. He did that for years right after your mother died. He wanted to speak—wanted his revenge." She laughed. "I wasn't going to be the one to give it to him, but I couldn't live like that anymore."

Lillian shivered, knowing "he" was Samson. She swallowed tightly, wanting to hear more about how all of this had happened, but not wanting to ask questions.

"I wanted you to come to Magnolian. I knew he would bother you then—since you look so much like your mother. He couldn't have resisted." She smiled a twisted, angry smile straight at Lillian. "Sure enough, he did, but you found out what he wanted, and that was my undoing. I thought you might humor him for a couple months, and maybe he would go away or follow you or maybe that you would stay and he would be your problem. I'm not sure what I thought. I just didn't want to be hounded anymore." She sighed and put her hands together as if in prayer.

"Grand, I just have one question. Who hit me on the head, and who cut the brakes and poisoned me? Did you do all of that? I just don't see how you could have." She was still bewildered about those things. Grand didn't seem like she would have had the time to do all of it, let alone the strength.

"No. Timmy knocked you out. I had told him to do that if he saw you near the paths in the woods. He fears me, so he would and did do anything I told him to. He also cut the brakes when Percy wasn't around. That was easy for him." She grinned. "But the poison—that was my doing. I had morphine crystals from years ago when an old relative had cancer and stayed for hospice at Magnolian. I secreted them away, knowing they would eventually come to good use. Then I played the frail old woman in front of most, doing what I wanted when people weren't looking. It was a smart plan. It worked for years." She smiled, her upper lip curling with something that looked like pride.

"Did you mean to kill me with the morphine then?" Lillian gulped, bile rising in her throat.

"Oh, no, dear. I'm not stupid, and I don't want you dead. I love you, you know." She stopped and glanced at Lillian. "Anyway, I knew what the lethal dosage was. I just wanted to give you a warning about Samson—to stop nosing in things that didn't concern you." Grand's voice was hard like granite.

"So, you loved the house beyond any of us," Lillian whispered, still in disbelief. Her throat felt like it might close up at any moment.

"When it came to that, yes. I did. The house has stood and will stand for years to come while the rest of us die off." She grinned in pure joy, and the look was obviously sincere.

With that statement, Lillian realized that Grand was insane. There was no other explanation for it. It only made knowing what she did marginally easier. She rose to leave. She didn't know what else to say anyway right now.

"Grand, get some sleep now." Lillian knew there was no point in talking about what had happened. Grand had a point of view that had lasted for more than forty years. It wasn't going to change now.

As she was leaving the room, Aunt Lorelei walked in—all blue cotton and sandalwood fragrance. Lillian noticed she was actually wearing makeup as well. She looked different—as if she had been freed from some long captivity. She engulfed Lillian in a hug, and Lillian began to cry on her ample shoulder.

"I'm so sorry for not being there for you, Lillian. I knew something was wrong, but I didn't know what. I promise things will be different from here on out." She looked at Lillian with watery brown eyes and smiled a tiny smile. "I'll spell you in here. I think I can stay awake the rest of the night with her." She looked over at Grand.

"It's okay, Aunt Lorelei. It's been a confusing month or so. I'll see you in the morning." She walked out of the room and down the hall, expecting to see Will there, but he was gone.

Walking to the end of the hall where there was a window, she watched the snow fall under a pale moon, the ground illuminated like a light of its own. She decided to spend the night in the waiting room, not thinking she had a ride home anyway. After walking back to the empty waiting room, she collapsed into a chair and fell asleep.

Lillian awoke in the wee hours of morning, cold and shaky. An older man was sitting on the other side of the room, his head in his hands. Lillian wondered what his loss was. Will was sitting beside her, stroking her hair and calling her name. When she opened her eyes, he offered her a cup of coffee. She gratefully took it.

He looked at her with red-rimmed, tired eyes, and her heart plummeted in her chest. "I have to tell you some bad news, Lillian. I don't know any easy way to say it. Do you need a minute?" He held her hand as she woke up with the first few sips of coffee.

"No. Just tell me," her voice was a tired rasp. "I can take it." She rubbed her bleary eyes and leaned against him as he spoke.

He sighed. "Your Grand died suddenly last night. Aunt Lorelei had left the room to get some coffee when it happened." He filled her in on the details. The doctors determined that Grand had died of a sudden heart attack around one in the morning. The slight bruise on her head from being hit by the gun had nothing to do with it, they said. It was probably her history of heart trouble. The night had just been too much for her.

When he reached that part of the story, she patted his hand reassuringly. "I know they're right. You had to knock her out. She was—deranged. I think all I can do is remember Grand as she was when we laughed together. I have so many good memories." She smiled even as her lips trembled and salty tears fell on Will's red sweater. He went on to tell her more about Grand's death.

"The nurses said that they heard a blood curdling scream—their exact words—come from her room. When they rushed in, she was already dead. They said she looked scared to death. They were all pretty freaked out." His voice died as he looked at Lillian, who had grown pale.

"I think we know who was in that room. I wonder what he did to scare her that much." Lillian leaned into Will. She wasn't angry at Samson. She was just sad about all of the loss that had led up to this moment. She sat with Will for another moment, just listening to his slow and steady heartbeat. Then they walked slowly out of the hospital hand in hand. There were still so many things to do, Lillian thought as they got in the car and headed for Magnolian. The snow was still falling and had blanketed the ground in white.

Chapter 21

The nightingale, their only vesper-bell, sung sweetly to the rose the
day's farewell.
—Lord Byron

That night in Grand's hospital room was Samson's last visit, as far as Lillian knew, to anyone. She had not seen him or felt his presence at Magnolian in the two days since Grand's death. The house felt peaceful, and she was thankful for that.

Grand's funeral was a large affair at the Baptist Church with Brother Mark officiating the service. Dozens of flower arrangements were delivered and mourners gathered. Joe Tate and others had agreed out of respect for Grand not to publish the details that were coming to light about Samson Jones' disappearance. Everwood showed up en masse to mourn Beverly Stark, and Lillian's heart healed a bit at each murmur of things Grand had done to help someone who needed the help. All the teary eyes reassured her that there was something beyond the evil that Grand had done and that most would be appalled to find out about. She supposed there were two sides to most people, and the dark side was stronger in some than in others. That had certainly been the case with Grand, she mused as the line of those who paid their respects after the burial died down to a trickle. Her legs ached, and she longed to get back to Magnolian and into a hot bath. She was mentally and physically drained.

Will took her arm, and they left Ridgemont Cemetery, where the grass was still green, and pine branches swayed in the early December wind. Grand was buried on a slope with the rest of the Grangers and

Starks. The spot was under a huge, gnarled oak tree whose branches hung over the white marble markers as if in protection. Lillian took one last look at Grand's burial plot and at the silver casket poised over a green tarp and turned to walk away with Will.

They got into the car for the drive back to Magnolian, relieved to be out of the cold wind that signaled the coming winter. Will looked at Lillian, and she knew he wanted to say something. He had been quiet all morning since picking her up for the funeral.

"What is it? It's okay whatever it is." She smiled at him, resting her hand on his dark suit clad arm as he pulled out of the parking place near the cemetery gates.

"I'm just wondering—" he faltered.

"Go on." Her voice was steady.

"I'm wondering if you really want to stay at Magnolian." Will breathed a sigh as he spoke, signaling how hard it had been to say those words. He steered the car smoothly along Main Street under a snow white sky.

"Yes, I'm staying—at least for the next few days. There's one more thing I have to do. I have to go back to the woods and dig and see what we find. Samson's body needs to be laid to rest. I need to do that for him." She clenched her fists in determination on her lap.

"I understand. Does tomorrow work for you?" He looked at her, and she realized he was totally serious. How could she have doubted that he would be with her though this ordeal, too?

"Tomorrow after one. Meet me at Magnolian, and we'll go together. I have to go by your father's office first and talk the will over with him."

"It's a date." He put his hand on her knee and kept it there. She looked out the window, her throat hurting with unshed tears.

They were quiet on the rest of the drive home, Lillian crying a bit into a wadded up tissue and Will focused on the road. They pulled up in front of Magnolian, and she got out of the car.

She kissed him lightly on the lips. "Till tomorrow." She went inside and walked straight upstairs, turning only the sitting room light on. She peeled her black ankle-length dress off, brushed her teeth, and washed her face. Then she dropped into bed and tumbled into the void of sleep.

The next morning, clad in a velour jogging suit, she met with Grand's lawyer—Joe Tate. It was strange going to his office now after so much had passed between them since her first visit. She smiled at him as she went in, and he closed the door behind her.

He sighed heavily, "How are you, Lillian?" He looked at her, interested in her response. A lump lodged in her throat as she thought of all the bad things she had thought about him and even accused him of.

"I'm as well as can be expected, Joe. Thanks for asking." She smiled a half smile at him.

"Well, let's get down to business. I guess that's the only way." He crossed his hands behind his head and leaned back in his swivel chair. "Lillian, I'm glad all this hasn't gotten out about Beverly. Not many people know what happened in the woods the other night. I think it's best that way. She was a good woman as far as most people knew. I'd like to keep it that way. How about you?"

Lillian nodded, tears pooling in her eyes at his regard for Grand and his delicacy concerning the situation.

"As far as the will goes, though, she left you Magnolian. You've been named in the will for twenty years—almost since the time of your birth. There'll be no contesting it, of course, by anyone." He looked at her with pursed lips. "As it stands, though, you are free and clear to sell the house and land or whatever you want to do. It's yours. You can let your aunt stay or go. That's for you to decide. Beverly left her all of her jewelry, but that's it. You have everything else—the car, the money in the bank, the mutual funds she had, all of it. You're a rich young lady, Lillian." He leaned forward, crossing his arms on his desk and giving her a small smile.

"Whew. This is a lot to digest," Lillian said, pushing her hair back with both hands and looking at him. "But it's also good news," she smiled. "And I know my aunt will be staying on at Magnolian—as long as she wants to. I don't want her to go." She took a deep breath.

"All right, well, all that's left to do is transfer some things into your name, and you got some papers to sign." He held a pen out to her.

She signed the forms, the only the sound in the room the pen scratching for a few minutes, and smiled at him. "Thanks for everything, Joe."

"Sure thing, Lillian. I'll do anything I can to help you further. Just say the word." He smiled at her, and she knew he meant it. She thought she was going to end up a lot closer to him than she had thought she ever would, especially since Will was in the picture.

As she left Joe Tate's office and walked through the cold to her car a few minutes later, her cell phone rang. It was Donovan.

Her smile faltering, she answered the phone, taking a deep breath.

"How are you, Bama girl?" Donovan's voice, full of warmth, made her a little sad.

"I'm okay. A lot has happened here in the past few days, though." Her eyes welled up again with tears. She wondered how many she had left to cry.

She related the story to him, and he responded with silence, gasps, and murmurs throughout the telling of it. She grew quiet and cleared her throat.

"Do you need me to come down? Are you coming back? Is there anything I can do?" he asked in a rush as she reached her car, leaning against it, the phone up to her ear.

"Donovan, I appreciate everything you've done for me. You have been one of the best friends I've ever had." Her voice shook with the truth of that statement. "I know now that I'm not coming back to Pittsburgh, though. I'm going to stay here at Magnolian. I've inherited the house in Grand's will, and it just feels right to stay here. I think I can find a job in town and finish college and everything nearby. I just know it's the right thing to do. I can't really explain it, but I need to give back something here to the people who've lost so much because of what Grand did" She grew silent, and he did, too, for a moment.

When he spoke, she could hear the pain in his voice. "I can understand your decision. That place is part of you now, and it's your heritage—your inheritance. If you ever need me or anything, just call. I mean it, Lillian." She thought she could hear him sniff in the background, but she wasn't sure.

"I will, and Donovan?"

"Yes?" His voice was quiet.

"You can visit any time. Bring a guest if you'd like." She said the last bit and laughed, but he got her point.

"I will." He hesitated and continued, "I knew you and Will would be together, and that's good. I could see how you felt about him, and I knew I'd lost—lost you, I mean. But I'm really happy for you both, Lillian. I hope you find all the happiness you both deserve. I know it's been pretty rough so far." He said this softly, his voice dying near the end of the statement, as she remembered it often did when he was touched by something.

"Thanks, Donovan. You have no idea how much that means to me." She brushed a tear away, her voice shaking a little.

"Keep in touch now, and I will, too, friend," he said. She could hear the smile in his voice as she clicked end.

She pulled into the drive to Magnolian, and Will drove up a few minutes later. They had one last thing to do to put the ghosts of Magnolian to rest.

Chapter 22

*The sunrise wakes the lark to sing, The moonrise wakes the
nightingale. Come, darkness, moonrise, everything That is so silent,
sweet, and pale: Come, so ye wake the nightingale.*
—Christina Rossetti

Lillian stood in front of the house—just looking up at it, thinking
this is mine. And what will I do with it? The house looked somehow
bereft to her under the blank, white sky. It had looked that way since
Grand's death. Perhaps spring would change that, or maybe it would
just take making the house her own to change it.

Percy Jones walked around the side of the house just as Will got
out of his car. Percy was carrying a shovel and other supplies. His
face was somber, but there was a light in his eyes that had not been
there before. He was going to claim his son and put his body to rest
finally, after all these years. At least, that was the hope. When Lillian
had told him the night before right here in the front yard about her
talk with her grandmother and about the events that had transpired
near the water tower, he had gone white and trembled. He had needed
to go sit on the porch swing to collect himself, he was so shaken.
Once he had caught his breath, she had asked him if he wanted to go
with her and look for Samson's body. He had said "yes" with tears in
his eyes. She had hugged him hard and told him she had asked Will to
go, too, so they could all do it together.

The three of them walked is silence around the house and toward
the path in the woods. The sun shined against the white sky, a pale
orb floating in milk, and a slight breeze blew through the trees,

rustling them as if they whispered so many secrets. Birds chirped and fluttered through the yard, looking for each other in the almost winter afternoon. The grass crunched under their feet as they approached the head of the trail. Rays of sun shone down in a V shape around the opening, and the dust motes and other tiny particles in the air danced in the light. They walked through the rays and on to the path. After some minutes, they reached the water tower. Its menace was gone, and no longer would this place be one of sorrow. Lillian could feel that even as they reached the tower. She and Will stood back a bit and let Percy go to the spot that was marked, as she had told him it would be and had been for days now. When she had told him about her grandmother's role in the whole thing, he had grown sad and somber. He told her, "I know she cared for me and for him. She just couldn't see things happen like that. I'm angry, but I won't leave Magnolian. My heart's here, and now I am finding my child probably is, too." Lillian had hugged him hard, letting tears fall on his flannel shirted shoulder. But that was yesterday. Today was a new day.

Finding the large stick that was still marking the spot where Samson Jones's bones lay, Percy began digging in the cold ground. Will took over for him when he was overcome with emotion. He dug in silence for a few minutes, stopping occasionally to wipe sweat off of his brow with a handkerchief. When Will hit something with a thunk of the shovel, Percy took the shovel again and sifted the sand. They found the remains of Samson Jones wrapped in a red blanket. Percy knelt to the ground and wept harsh sobs as Will and Lillian held each other a few feet away. After a few minutes, Will and Percy picked up the red blanket and its sad contents, wrapping them in another blanket he had brought for that purpose, and began to walk back down the path toward Magnolian. Lillian walked beside them, wiping tears from her eyes. They took Samson's remains to the back and put the blanket down in the garden. Lillian went inside to call Joe Tate and the police department to report their findings.

After the authorities had questioned the three of them outside and gone, Will and Lillian stood in the front yard, holding each other tightly.

"So, this is it, huh? What's next?" Will asked into her hair, and Lillian could hear the tightness of his voice.

"Nowhere. I'm staying. I'm the new mistress of the manor," Lillian said, standing on her toes to press her lips to his. "I guess next is that we get a proper burial done for Samson—here on the grounds—maybe right by the head of the path there since that's where he and Gretchen used to meet." She smiled, but her lips trembled.

"I think that would be the best way to honor his memory—and hers, as long as Percy agrees," Will said softly, kissing her fully on the lips as the breeze stirred the trees and leaves around them.

They turned to walk into the house, and on the edge of her line of sight to the right, Lillian imagined she saw a shape in the yard some distance from them, but it was only a shimmer of sunlight on a solitary tree.

THE END

WWW.LISALGREER.COM

ABOUT THE AUTHOR

Lisa Greer is a college English instructor and online lead writing tutor who makes her home in Brownsville, Texas. She holds a M.A. degree in Eighteenth-Century British Literature from the University of Alabama at Birmingham. She also owns Gothicked (http://gothicked.blogspot.com), a blog that reviews gothic romance novels and other gothic novels. *Magnolian* is her debut novel. Find her on Facebook at Lisa Greer Author and on Twitter at Gothicked.

BookStrand

www.BookStrand.com

CPSIA information can be obtained at www.ICGtesting.com
Printed in the USA
BVOW04s1003120614

356196BV00018B/298/P